Cambridgeshire Libraries & Information Service
This book is due for return on or before the latest date shown
above, but may be renewed up to three times if the book is not
in demand. Ask at your local library for details.
Please note that charges are made on overdue books.

LIBRARY

PJS

07090 75251 6742 2X

Last Stage to Hellfire

Behind Duke Montana lay a desperate manhunt, a murderous shootout and the mystery of a beautiful woman whose disappearance threatened the future of the entire territory.

Ahead of him was Hellfire and an even greater peril in the form of a gang of killers intent on finding the missing girl first, a dedicated lawman who hated him on sight, and beautiful Bella from his colourful past. It was she who posed the greatest danger of all.

Special agent Montana was used to living on the edge. But before the last of the gunsmoke drifted away from the deadly streets of Hellfire, he would know what it was like to dice with death especially with the game rigged for him to lose!

Last Stage to Hellfire

Dempsey Clay

A Black Horse Western

ROBERT HALE · LONDON

© Dempsey Clay 2004
First published in Great Britain 2004

ISBN 0 7090 7525 1

Robert Hale Limited
Clerkenwell House
Clerkenwell Green
London EC1R 0HT

Typeset by
Derek Doyle & Associates, Liverpool.
Printed and bound in Great Britain by
Antony Rowe Limited, Wiltshire

CHAPTER 1

BELLA AND THE DUKE

All was skeleton still.

The red-eyed lizard crouched motionless by the slab of ochre-colored rock with its hideous head cocked to one side and every sense alert as it attempted to identify the faint rustling sound from below ground, when suddenly the goshawk perched in the dead tree above emitted a small sharp cluck of alarm and flew away to the north.

The lizard was gone in a blink.

Stillness reasserted its total supremacy over the landscape for several minutes more before the tall figure appeared abruptly from the rocky jaws of Prairie Valley close by. Distorted at first by the heat haze of the last day of the plains' Indian summer, the silhouette slowly took on the lean shape of the man striding purposefully back along the faint trail he'd followed south into the valley two days earlier.

There was no eye here, neither animal or human, to note how starkly the swinging walk and impressive carriage contrasted with unshaven jowls and tattered garb. The fancy boots broken by rocky miles and the ripped trousers and blood-spattered shirt all attested to a man down on his uppers, yet how often did one encounter a bum who walked so much like the leader of the pack?

The man came on, then swung off the track by the dead tree to make his way directly across to the yellowed slab of stone that had attracted the lizard's attention.

Without a moment's hesitation he hunkered down to work his fingers beneath the leading edge, then sharply flipped the slab aside to expose the black hole beneath.

Something whipped up into the sunlight in a blur of mottled color, the sound of the deadly rattle a strident alarm bell that sent the man tumbling desperately backwards even as his right hand whipped out the tied-down Colt .45 faster than any timber rattler could blink.

The bullet head was darting forward when the gun exploded at point-blank range, leaving the headless body, all black and yellow and hideously beautiful, convulsing violently, gouting dark blood, turning its livid belly to the sun.

Duke Montana was generally not much for cussing but he was raging like a muleskinner as he scrambled to his feet and backed up several paces, waiting for the big thick body of the northern timber rattlesnake to go still, gun echoes slowly muttering away into distant silences.

'Sonuva!' he panted, sleeving his brow. Who expected rattlers this far north this late in the season? And immediately, right on cue, the inner voice which gave him far too much trouble – particularly when on assignment – whispered: *You raise hell, you've got to expect hell to hit back now and again, high-roller!*

He told his inner self to shut up, reached out gingerly with the toe of his ruined right boot and kicked the headless body aside.

He approached the hole warily. No more snakes. Hunkering down he reached in to grasp the steel handle of the high-quality carpetbag which he flipped out into the sunlight.

He sniffed.

The bag gave off a faint aroma of horse-sweat and malt whiskey blended subtly with a whiff of shaving-cream and pomade. The way he figured, it had been the bag's scents and welcoming texture which had first attracted the reptile, which then realized its plush surface would make an ideal bed for its winter hibernation.

Every movement brisk and efficient now, he quickly unzipped the bag and drew out a metal water canteen and a colored handtowel of fine linen. He swallowed half the contents of the canteen, then wet the towel sparingly and began scrubbing five days of dust and sweat from face, neck and hands.

That was as much as he could spare. Water was scarce down here in the low country this time of year.

The rest of him could stay dirty until he hit Hellfire, even if he hated going dirty worse than God hates sin.

Ablutions completed, he shucked off everything down to the long johns, which although well grimed showed the cut and style of high quality.

From the bag now came a carefully folded three-piece suit, starched white shirt, string tie and dapper Stetson, which had to be punched back into shape. And last but not least, handmade boots of finest Mexican leather.

By the time he'd finished dressing and squirting himself liberally with fragrance from a small spray bottle, he smelt and looked like the best-dressed gent one might encounter on the streets of Dodge, Wichita or even at his destination, the roaring mountain mining town of Hellfire.

A brisk hour's walk took him to the stage trail where it looped wide around the big bend of Mulroney's Creek. He set down his bag, tugged a heavy gold Waltham watch from his vest pocket, checked the time, grunted in satisfaction and turned his head to stare south-west. A tiny ball of hoof-kicked dust was heading his way.

For the first time in five days of hard riding, hair-raising close calls and deadly gunplay, Duke Montana let himself relax just a little. Prairie Valley had seen him lose his horse to a badman's bullet, kill a man hell bent on killing him, and have another he should have killed escape.

The bright side was the strong lead he'd got from a dying badman that Hellfire was the most likely place to search for a lovely young woman on the run before a bunch of killers found her first.

The coach and six came round the loop with a flourish, trailing a fluttering banner in its slipstream proclaiming this to be the very last run the company would be making from Henningwood and points south-east up to the high country and Hellfire.

His luck was holding, Duke told himself as the driver hit the brakes. Had he missed this run he could have faced a forty-mile hike, and he detested walking.

The Concord lurched to a dusty halt and curious faces stared down from the windows and the box.

'You travellin', mister?' It was the gun guard's last day after several years on the run, but he knew he'd never encountered this kind of flash along the hard-bitten track from Henningwood to Hellfire.

'You've got it,' Montana grinned, tossing his carpetbag high. 'Catch!'

All passengers but one stared curiously as the well-dressed figure swung inside out of the flooding sunlight. The drummer from Denver, the preacher from Heaven – if you believed his spiel – his lady wife who'd complained bitterly at every bump, lurch, jolt and shudder over the past fifty miles, plus the hard-faced man with the black mustache evidently accompanying the shapely blonde in the big picture hat – all fell silent as they checked him out with interest, which was nothing less than Montana expected.

But typically his attention was taken solely by the blonde, or what he could see of her, that was.

She was seated in the far corner, alongside the

black mustache, facing the horses. Montana looked her over admiringly as the drummer shifted to make room for him, noting the splendid figure, the latest Paris-style skirt and beaded jacket – and he was a man who knew his *haute couture*. He approved totally of the flamboyant hat even if it was preventing him getting a glimpse of her face, noted admiringly that the right hand drawing something slowly from her elegant black pocket-book sported some fine-looking jewellery. There was no sign of a ring on the fourth finger of her left hand which held the pocket-book.

'Ladies, gents,' he said amiably, removing his hat as he got comfortable. 'Montana's the name, Duke Montana. Gold's my game and I'm heading up to Hellfire to see if—'

'There's a hole deep enough to bury you in, you double-dealing piece of dirt. Say your prayers, shyster!'

It was the blonde with the pocket book and concealing hat who spoke. Only the hat wasn't concealing a thing any longer, and Duke Montana found himself staring into the angry face of a woman he'd loved and very definitely lost two years ago in Kansas City.

'Bella—' he began, then broke off. The preacher's wife emitted a gasp of sheer terror as she pointed a trembling finger at his ex-lover, and Duke paled when he saw why. Bella Duvall – who'd briefly but memorably once been his Bella – was holding a familiar-looking pearl-handled Saturday Night Special two-shot derringer in her steady hand, was

10

deliberately cocking the trigger with her pretty thumb.

It was seldom Montana found himself totally at a loss. His real occupation – and not even Belle Duvall had uncovered it during three memorable months together in Kansas City – was a highly dangerous one, and he was no stranger to desperate situations. But the reality that this was Bella, that she had every right to be blazing mad, plus the fact that he was probably incapable of hurting any woman – all ganged up on him in that long frozen moment as he actually feared his final hour had come.

'B-Bella,' he got out. Goddamnit, her finger was whitening on the trigger as everybody in the coach seemed to freeze into immobility. 'Honey – beautiful, I can explain. I had to run out on you. Your life was in danger. They'd have killed you if I'd stayed with you a day longer.'

The fact that his words were all solid truth appeared to have no effect. This was plainly a woman scorned, and everyone including a by now pale-faced Montana was bracing for the worst when the tall man seated at Belle's side bought in.

He snatched the gun from her hand and held it out of reach in one deft motion.

Bella's reaction was fast and furious. She slapped the man's face, clutched at the hand holding the two-shot – fumbled and missed.

Instantly Montana's heart began to beat again.

The signs were crystal clear.

Had fiery Bella been serious there was no way she could have been disarmed so easily.

11

It was a sign. He believed. He was goddamn saved!

The stage clattered noisily over a culvert as it began to climb. It was the only sound as five wide-eyed passengers, including a slow-smiling Montana dabbing at the fine film of cold sweat sheening his face, waited to see what she might do next.

What she eventually did, was smile.

'Thanks, Buck,' she told the black mustache. She reached out and squeezed his hand. 'I guess I only meant to scare him anyway. He scares quite easily, you know, although you'd probably guess that just by the way he dresses.'

Montana sat up straight and even smiled.

And thought: nothing unusual here. From a duel to the death in the valley, he'd cannoned headlong into his turbulent past. High drama and duty one moment, broad farce the next – yet again. This seemed to be the unchanging pattern of his life. And the sobering thought: was this how he would be remembered after he was gone? Dangerman and playboy?

Then he sighed and relaxed. Did all that really matter a damn just so long as he'd seemingly weathered the storm. And Bella had never been a woman to be taken lightly, as he knew only too well. She had beauty, brains and a bad temper, the last anything but least.

He felt so philosophical he didn't turn a hair when, calm and seemingly in full control now, Bella smiled sweetly and slipped in the knife.

'You see, my happy travelling-companions, this double-dealing dandy treated me very badly once –

vowed he loved me and promised me the world, then ran off with a naked strumpet half his age.' The memory seemed to bite. Flaring green eyes found his. 'And I warned him what would happen if I ever saw his smarmy smile again – you low-life, snake-in-the-grass bastard—'

'Oh, Cyrus!' gasped the preacher's wife. 'Such language. My smelling salts!'

By the time she'd been revived and the rocking Concord was bowling along freely like a big-hipped cucaracha dancer, the crew above totally unaware of the drama below, a kind of calm had been restored. And when the Saturday Night Special disappeared inside Buck Ramont's jacket, Montana smoothly produced something from an inside pocket of his tailored, four-button jacket.

It was a deck of cards.

Everyone stared incredulously as he leaned forward and extended the pack to Belle Duvall. He winked.

'This always settled you down whenever you got fractious, as I recall, honey. Go on, pick a card. Any card.'

Every eye was on Belle Duvall yet she only had eyes for Montana now – eyes from which all the fury of a woman scorned seemed to take for ever first to fade, then to dim, then at last disappear altogether.

He knew he was either being totally forgiven, or else she was adroitly concealing her bloody-minded intention to shoot him through the back of the head at the very first opportunity. With Bella a man could never be sure.

With all the grace of a duchess reaching for a canapé, she reached out and selected a card.

'Two of hearts?' guessed Montana.

'Why, yes it is, you four-flushing—'

'That's us, Belle,' he overrode her, his smile inviting the others to share the moment. 'Two of hearts, the lovers' card. And isn't this something, folks? This wonderful lady and I were torn apart by circumstances and thought we'd lost one another for ever. Yet now, out of a clear blue sky, destiny has brought us back together again. Who's got a drink to celebrate the occasion?'

The rum-dum drummer clutched his bottle to his skinny chest protectively. He wasn't sharing with anyone. But maybe they didn't need it. Judging by the relieved smiles all around it was plain everybody was well on the way towards accepting the fact that what had been witnessed was nothing more than a lovers' quarrel.

Ramont was one exception, and looked anything but accepting as he leaned forward to fix Montana with a frosty stare.

'Seems to me I need to know more about just what the hell happened in Kansas City, dude. Bella's my gal and business partner, and I reckon I got the right.'

'Please, Buck,' she said softly. Ramont shook her hand from his shoulder. He was big, strong in the shoulders, packed iron. And very plainly he didn't like one single thing about Duke Montana.

'I'm waiting,' he growled. 'Talk up.'

Montana sighed. He'd recognized the breed on

14

sight. Trouble. He might have been diplomatic, but the rigors of the past twenty-four hours had left him short on diplomacy and long on tetchiness.

'Why don't you go and—' he began, but Bella cut him off.

'Enough!' she snapped with that authority he remembered so well. She rested a hand on Ramont's arm and squeezed tight, shot a warning look at Duke. 'I was foolish to start this, but now it's finished. Period!' She stared imperiously from one to the other, and Montana felt that old familiar feeling as he met the impact of her eyes again. Memories . . . 'Agreed?'

'Hell . . . agreed.' He grinned, reaching for his cigarillos. 'What say you, boyfriend?'

Ramont scowled, muttered a curse, then shrugged and leaned back with a growl.

'OK, Belle, agreed. For now.'

Duke lighted up, then turned his attention to the landscape blurring past mica windows. After several miles which saw them top out the plateau and go bowling across it with the LAST STAGE TO HELLFIRE banner flapping in the backdraft, he realized Bella appeared genuinely to have calmed – snuggling up to tall, dark and dumb and leaving him free to focus on his assignment.

He hoped to find a missing woman in Hellfire. No, not for the predictable reason. This was a special woman and he had a special reason for wanting to find her. In truth it was his job.

Duke Montana had hopes of locating a Miss Hannah North in the mining town. High hopes.

Then he thought again. To be honest, his hopes weren't really all that high. It was more that he needed to find her than that he expected to. To be even more honest, it wasn't so much hope as a slim gambler's hunch that found him riding the last stage up from the plains. But as an old gambling pal, currently doing time in Leavenworth, often said, 'if you don't play your hunches what have you got?'

He frowned and made an admission.

He was really riding a long shot, and knew it. But what choice did he have? Had he been able to question that gunman he'd shot in the valley before he died, he might well have had himself a genuine lead on the whereabouts of this particular missing person, upon whose recovery or loss might hinge the entire future of the Territory.

Eventually he quit thinking and leaned back with a blanked mind, trying to keep his drifting gaze away from Bella's silk-sheathed ankles. Until a bellow from the box warned that their destination was in sight for all passengers riding what was ringingly proclaimed as 'The last stage to Hellfire!' Which now, for some reason, to the ear of a suddenly bone-weary Duke Montana, seemed to carry a vaguely ominous ring.

CHAPTER 2

LAWMAN OF
HELLFIRE

Dead on three o'clock in the morning Duke Montana sat bolt upright in the premier suite of the Territory Hotel and breathed, 'Dimitri!'

Slowly the dregs of sleep began to fade and, buck naked and peeved, he swung his feet to the rich pile and stumbled out on to the balcony, fuzzily coming to realize he'd been dreaming. Yet it was not so much as a dream, so he realized as he dropped his hands to the railing and shook his tousled head, than a reliving of something that had actually happened – and it had happened at Prairie Valley.

It seemed he could still hear an echo of that whispering voice. So he cursed aloud and it disappeared. Now it was totally silent, as any night should be at this ungodly hour, even in a roaring mining town.

He'd turned in early, something he did roughly twice a year, upon realizing that his long hunt, culminating in the shoot-out in Prairie Valley and topped off by his twenty-mile hike back to the stage trail, had drained him and left him tetchy and groggy, which was no way for a tough operator in his specialized line of work to feel.

He squinted at the cloud-shadowed moon and massaged the back of his neck. Hellfire, a bona fide rip of a town if ever he'd seen one, had at last put up the shutters sometime during the five to six hours he'd been asleep.

Before him stretched an unnaturally silent land-scape of a town sprawled on either side of its mint-new railroad tracks. The secret and shadowed yards and gardens flanking the buildings on this, the better side of town, appeared mysterious and even romantic under that old moon. But these attractions were eventually swallowed by the brash falsefronts and yellow Rager lamps of the main street two blocks west. The deserted street was lined on either side by emaciated hand-planted trees that appeared to be pining for life in the great green woods far from the feverish heat and clamor of lust, greed and grief that generated the atmosphere of every boomtown he'd ever seen, and he'd seen his share.

A chill from the hills touched his bare chest driving him back through the french windows into his moon-shadowed room.

He stood staring at the rumpled bed, recalling the dream and again envisioned a dying gunman invok-ing the name: 'Dimitri.'

He scratched the back of his neck. What the hell kind of a name was that anyway? But that was surely

18

what Wade had said, and they said dying men never lie.

Passing up his cigars, he located a packet of Turkish cigarettes on the nightstand. He leaned a shoulder against the french doors and lit up, his thoughts running deep and sober.

Killing in the line of duty rarely troubled him. You couldn't allow it to. And Joe Wade had begged for it. He'd been a rider on the wrong side of the law. . . .

The trail that led him eventually to Prairie Valley had taken him from the Stone Sisters to Timberlake, Murch Hill, Dix City and Shackertown, a lot of places and a lot of miles. But he'd stuck to the hunt, convinced this as-yet unnamed trio had recently visited Cascade County where they'd been asking after the woman he was searching for, whose name was Hannah North.

It was a long shot, this difficult pursuit through some of the roughest country in the region. He knew it, but figured he had little choice after three weeks spent in futile searching for a woman so pretty she should have stood out like a beacon, but seemingly hadn't done so. If this trio, described to him by one informant as 'mean and proddy-lookin' as a passel of wild range bulls', had come up with anything on the elusive Hannah North then he wanted to know about it. He also meant to uncover the reason for their interest, for that young woman had connections and a history linking her to people and events which just might, in time, shake the very foundations of the Territory.

The tracks ultimately brought him to a hole-in-the-wall cave in the immense cliff face which ran the entire twenty-mile length of the valley's western side.

He was tempted to tie up the horse a mile from the cliffs and infiltrate afoot but realized he was by then punch-drunk and rubber-legged from fatigue. So he rode in closer. This proved a mistake due to the chance happening that saw one of the trio quit the hideout on dusk to shoot something for the pot, something he was unaware of until almost too late.

It proved easy enough to make his stealthy way unobserved quite close to the camp, where he sought the cover of a black boulder which stood almost within hearing distance of the black outlines of two men standing by a cheerful camp-fire drinking coffee laced with gin and feeding pine cones to the flames.

It was his first close glimpse of two of his quarry and they fitted his expectations to a T, one silhouette lithe and supple-looking with twin guns buckled around his hips, the other – Wade as he was to learn – short and stocky with a shock of hair that caught the fireglow as he leaned lazily on a rifle.

Desperadoes. If that wasn't their brand then he was no judge. He must get closer. The cliff lay deeply shadowed in back of his boulder and he was about to ease in that direction when the faint but unmistakable sound of a snapping twig caused his stomach to take a dive.

Someone was in back of him and coming his way!

From there his prudent plan simply to check out the bunch and maybe get a line on their interest in

20

Hannah North, came apart like ragweed in a Texas twister.

Unwilling to lock horns with three gun-hellions at the end of punishing days in the saddle, the man whom some called the Duke found himself with just two simple objectives as he ducked low and went streaking away through the tiger-stripe bars of light and shadow that patterned the ground between the scatter of canted stones. Get to his horse and get gone. Fast.

He moved fast and quiet to put an uneventful hundred yards behind him before a big bass voice breached the night's calm.

'Heads up, boys, we got company! And there he goes!'

The tail-end of the shout was swallowed by the bellow of a rifle that sent Montana diving headlong as lead powdered stone close by.

He was up and running in an instant, fleet-footed as a mountain goat and showing no trace of exhaustion now as he sliced into the trees and zigzagged for the hollow where he'd stashed the horse.

The hollow was empty. The horse was a rental from Dobie Creek and the gunfire had caused it to take fright and break away. Following the bent grass, Montana took after the animal and by a small miracle caught up with it minutes later in a box draw. As he filled leather and snatched up the broken reins he heard the stutter of running boots and glimpsed the burly figure as the man vaulted a deadfall and came straight for him.

His sixshooter bucked; the hardcase dived wildly

for cover and rolled away into darkness.

Duke used spur.

He'd covered some fifty racing yards when two dark shapes loomed directly ahead, all three caught momentarily in open grassland.

Guns flared orange and wicked from both directions and Montana kicked clear as his horse went down in slow motion with a .32 slug in its brain. Enraged yet ice-cool, he hit ground fanning gun hammer.

Ragged and shrill through the voice of his Colt came the scream and he saw the figure crash to its back, big hat rolling free like a cartwheel.

Instantly the second man shouted something and vanished into the trees, the sounds of flight rapidly fading until Duke's sharp ears picked up the beat of horses starting up and quickly breaking into a gallop; the sounds of flight faded swiftly into dark distances.

He lay shadow-still and barely seeming to breathe. He forced himself not to move for a full five minutes before rising with a sixgun cocked and ready in each hand. The sounds of moaning and a feeble rustling in the grass led him to the fallen man.

He'd been struck square in the chest. Eyes glittering with total hatred blazed up at him from the bloodied grass.

'Dirty, stinkin' dry-gulcher . . .'

Montana holstered. No further need of guns here. This one's life was hanging by a thread.

'Who are you, and what's your interest in Hannah North?' he demanded.

'A dirty range dick . . . I shoulda guessed. Well, my pards will get you for this, you mongrel dog. They'll get square for old Joe Wade, you'll see . . .' His voice faded and he began to weep. 'Dimitri . . .' he breathed, then went still, face to the rising moon.

His cigarette had gone out.

Duke shook his head and crossed to the bureau to take out a silk robe. He drew it on then made a light. The dark had been spooking him and he knew that this, like the dream, was a sure sign that he'd been burning both ends of the candle too brightly for too long.

He was behind schedule, he'd killed a man, almost touched off another shooting aboard the stage, and was next door to certain that, if he didn't knuckle down here in Hellfire and get on with the job there'd be trouble from the people who kept Duke Montana in Cuban cigars, Godfather's Louisiana Bourbon and fine suites in top-flight hotels.

Then his jaw set in stubborn lines and he thought – to hell with them anyway!

He needed some stand-down time. But anyone who knew him – such as, say, beautiful Bella, for instance – would understand that when he thought relaxation the very last thing he had in mind was rest. As with just about everything else that distinguished him from those worthy citizens he was often called upon to help or protect, the Duke relaxed in his own way.

The eye-catching sign above the long, low-roofed, stone-and-hardwood building with the steel-barred windows, read simply but proudly:

HELLFIRE LAW OFFICE
Conway Dunstan: Sheriff

The sheriff of Hellfire liked to stand off a ways across Wagon Street and admire that fine sign of his at odd times. Such as when he might be busting with pride because things were going really well, or those other times when, hidden behind his craggy features, silver sheriff's star and the worn leather vest he wore both summer and winter, he privately feared his town might be headed for Hell in a handbasket.

Today it was an uneasy amalgam of both points of view that found the mining town's lean lawman standing out there in the early sun, massaging his jaw and looking thoughtful while pedestrians, riders, a wagonload of hairy Cousin Jack miners heading back up into the Dogwood Hills, and even the undertaker's somber coach and six black horses, were all forced to go round him.

Dunstan wasn't deliberately reminding Hellfire's three thousand citizens who was in charge by commanding the middle of the main street this way, but neither did he like them to forget it. Not any one of them.

Then he heard it:

'Momma, why's the man standing in the street thataway? Is he lost?'

The lawman turned sharply. The young widow looked apologetic; the freckle-faced kid holding her hand seemed genuinely puzzled as he squinted up at his tall figure.

'Sorry, Sheriff.' The woman smiled. 'You know

what children are like.'

Fortunately, the bachelor lawman had no idea. He was married to his job. But the interruption reminded him of duty waiting. So he touched hatbrim grudgingly, shot the kid a hard look and headed east along Wagon to begin his first patrol of the day.

Hellfire was a mining town with no ambitions to be anything else. Standing on a plateau in the lower hills around two miles from the aspen, maple and oak slopes of the Dogwood Hills where the first hairy miner had turned over the first chunk of gold-veined rock a decade earlier, the sheriff's town was solid, raffish, noisy, energetic, prosperous and, in his view at least, far too wild and loose-living for its own good.

As he turned from Wagon into St Leque now, Dunstan could see two saloons, the Indian Queen and Golden Nugget, and one clapboard honkytonk where – it was a well known fact of life – you could pay the girls to do more than just dance with you.

Dunstan sniffed.

He was no puritan, or so he claimed. But from where he stood behind his five-pointed star he could envision a hundred ways the town could upgrade itself without too severely eroding its well-earned reputation for hell-raising.

A stocky gentleman with a flashy gold watch-chain stretched tight across his fully packed weskit strode by with a fuming cigar sticking out of his face, threw him a salute and wished him top of the morning.

Dunstan turned and spat.

Lease agents! He reckoned nine out of ten of that breed now in his town were crooked, based on the number of cases he had to deal with involving claim jumping, forged licences, bogus assays and a hundred and one evils associated with those leeches who made life far more difficult than it need be for the mostly simple-hearted miners and prospectors who merely wanted to get rich quick, if only the crooks and parasites would let them.

He halted on meeting the righteously stern eye of a man who, as far as he understood, shared his notions on exactly how fine any town, county or territory could be if it really tried.

The face on the colored poster tacked to the telegraph pole was twice life-sized and the message in twelve inch letters beneath exhorted the citizens of Hellfire to VOTE SENATOR NATHAN T. SINGLE-MAN for GOVERNOR!

The territorial elections were months away but Singleman was campaigning already. His Democrat rival was making capital of a number of shady political and commercial enterprises the senator had allegedly been involved in, and Singleman would, according to the pundits, need to make every post a winner if he wanted to take over in Capital City.

Singleman was popular with conservatives like the sheriff but wildly out of touch with men like Benny the Bum, who accosted Dunstan as he paused to consider the display of mining equipment in the windows of Goodpasture's Emporium.

But it was justice, not politics, that prompted ragged young Benny to approach his natural enemy this morning.

'Shurf, I want to know what you aim to do about

Chett Wilson,' he declared, swaying just a little in the breeze.

'What do you mean . . . do about him? What's he done now?'

'Barred me from the Palace again.'

'Wonder why?'

'I'm serious, Sheriff. All I done was touch her.'

Dunstan arched an eyebrow.

'Who?'

Benny's cheerful, booze-ridden young face shone.

'Her, of course. Ain't you seen her yet? She come in yesterday on the stage. You know, the one the preacher's wife has been gripin' about.' He threw skinny arms wide. 'The goddess. Miss Bella Duvall. I reckon I'm in love, and that varmint Wilson had the nerve to kick me out. . . . Hey, where you goin', Sheriff? I ain't through yet.'

The sheriff was.

He'd just been reminded of some unfinished business left over from the previous day, namely the incident alleged to have taken place aboard the last stage from the plains involving some flash stranger and a blonde 'singer and entertainer' whom the sheriff had only seen at a distance, and most definitely wanted to see again. Strictly in the line of business, of course.

Travelling back along the recently renamed Railroad Avenue, the lawman caught a glimpse of a symbol of the reason the stage company had been forced to shut down its operation out of Henningwood. A stubby black loco and tender were chugging to and fro beyond the railroad sheds, snorting, clanking and proclaiming changing times. The coming of the railroad just three months earlier had finally put the stage company out of business and burdened the sheriff with just one more potential source of trouble.

Railroads brought new-timers in droves, and not all were desirable.

Silleck hadn't come to town by train, but by the lawman's assessment he was about as undesirable as you could get.

The two-gunner was loafing on the porch of the Hot Chow eatery on the main street corner, a young man with old eyes who moved lightly, with the hint of coiled spring in his body. His skin was deep bronze, his hair coal-black, and he had a way of looking at a man as though measuring him up for a coffin.

Silleck was just one of a number of unwelcome newcomers to Hellfire in recent times who didn't seem to hold down steady jobs, yet were never short of spending silver. Who kept strange hours and had the kind of friends that had Dunstan looking them up in his Wanted files, but without much success thus far.

He'd forgotten the man by the time he reached the biggest, plushest and classiest saloon-cum-gambling-hall-cum-show-house in the hills.

The Silver Palace was barely stirring at this mid-morning hour. But a piano tinkled from a back bar as Dunstan strolled through the big casino room with a nod to a sleepy case-keeper, and there she was at the keyboard, playing and singing in a strong untrained soprano. Chett Wilson was leaning on the piano with a stogie clamped between his teeth, grinning, nodding approvingly and tapping time with his toe.

Bella Duvall seemed to have settled in real fast, and a man only needed one glance to understand why.

The music stopped. Dunstan removed his hat. The saloonkeeper scowled.

'Now what, Sheriff?' Wilson was surly. Peace officer and saloonkeeper shared a prickly relationship. One never drank and the other drank far too much. They nursed other differences and distinctions. But because Wilson respected the law, and Dunstan knew the man to be a straight shooter, they managed to get along well enough without any risk of ever getting to be friends. 'You sent a deputy along to tell me to hold the noise down after midnight, and I done it. What now? You're scared folks are just having too much fun here, mebbe? That'd really get up the nose of a killjoy like you, I reckon.'

Dunstan refused to rise to the bait, even though he suspected the other was talking big and blowy just to impress present company.

'Miss, er, Duvall. It is miss, isn't it?'

Bella proffered her hand and the lawman took it gingerly. He was staring. They said she was beautiful. They'd understated.

'What can I do for you, Sheriff?'

'Er, I didn't want to interrupt your act, Miss Duvall.'

'Bella,' she insisted. 'And you're not interrupting. Chett's heard enough, haven't you, Chett. Now you can go have a beer and decide if you want to hire Buck and me for your show, or not.' She dimpled sweetly. 'Can't you?'

'Can Buck dance as good as you say?'

'Even better. We were selling out every night in Fort West.'

'Er . . . well, guess I will go think it over, Miss Bella,' the saloonkeeper responded. He smiled lecherously at the woman and, with a parting scowl at Dunstan, was gone.

'It was nothing, Sheriff,' she said brightly, crossing one leg over the other with a sibilant swish of silk. 'A joke, as a matter of fact. The gun thing with Mr Montana, that is. That's a running gag. We're old friends with our funny ways.' Her brow puckered. 'You have come to see me about what happened on the stage, haven't you?'

He had indeed. But by the time he'd listened to her version of events he was beginning to wonder what the hell he was doing here. She was bright and high-spirited as well as stunning. Stood to reason that spirited and high-style women like this might prove a bit too much for dried-up old biddies like Preacher Nolan's frowzy wife.

'Well, reckon all that seems satisfactory,' he said at last, turning his hat in his hands. 'Of course I'll have to speak to your, er, friend, Mr . . . what did you say his name was? Oklahoma . . . ?'

'Montana, Duke Montana. Must you see him also, Sheriff?'

'Well, I guess. Any reason I shouldn't?'

'Oh no. He's a perfect gentleman and—'

'Some kind of gambling dude, I hear tell.'

'Yes,' she said guardedly. 'I suppose he would

30

strike some as that sort. But actually he's a business-man who just likes to gamble. Shares, stocks and shares. He's quite respectable.'

'The Nolans don't seem to think so, Miss, er, I mean, Bella.'

'I can assure you Duke Montana is a perfect gentleman and—'

'And a solid citizen and pillar of the church to boot.'

Both turned at the voice as Montana appeared beneath the arch, removing his hat as he smiled at Bella and scowled at the law.

'I'm Duke Montana, Sheriff. What can I do for you?'

The sheriff said his piece as he sized up his man. His first impression was that Montana, dapper in tailored broadcloth suit with a waisted coat and flared lapels, was a typical high-roller, good-looking, groomed and far too confident for his own good. He then noted the way the panels of the waisted jacket were tailored to flare smoothly over twin sixguns in tooled leather holsters string-tied low on the thighs, and was forced to reassess.

Another one?

Why had his town in recent times seemed to have begun to bristle with the gunpacking breed, where in the past mostly the worst he'd had to contend with were roaring miners on the ran-tan, domestic disputes, the occasional knifing or shooting – mostly over money or women – and any number of rafter-rattling but essentially harmless brawls?

Surely he couldn't blame the trains for it all. This

one had come by stage.

'You see,' Bella said reassuringly when Dunstan finally fell silent. 'Old friends.' She slipped an arm through Montana's to prove the point. 'Of course, I suppose it was a little too much, me pulling our old "Glad to see you, hands up!" trick we used to amuse ourselves with in Sun City, Duke. But I'm sure the sheriff understands now. Don't you, Sheriff?'

Quitting the place a short time later, Dunstan found himself in an unsettled state of mind. The woman was a dazzler and he was strongly inclined to believe what she said, most of it anyway. Yet because lawmen were suspicious by nature, he wondered if Bella Duvall might not be just a tad over-attractive, plausible and charming.

As for Montana – that was one he would look up on in his files. Anybody who walked that tall, packed iron like it was part of his wardrobe, admitted to being a serious gambler and who was plainly some kind of ladies' man, just had to have raised hell or stepped on the toes of the law someplace.

The office's comprehensive files revealed nothing on one Mr Duke Montana of no known address. For some reason, instead of this setting Conway Dunstan's suspicions to rest, the total absence of any information, either good or bad, only fanned his concerns. As a consequence he promised himself to keep a sharp eye on Bella's flash friend until he quit town. Which with any luck might prove to be sooner rather than later.

CHAPTER 3

THE DUDE
MUST DIE

A pallid yellow sun was hanging cold in the western sky as the man named Silleck rode back up from the valley and headed for the hills. His runty black mustang had the stamina of all its wild breed and he was making good time as he followed the now defunct stage trail from Mulroney's Creek across the plain to Marvinville, where he stopped off for beer and cheese at that one-horser's clapboard saloon and way station.

He wasn't known here but they read his brand plain enough. Trouble. As a consequence both boozers and barkeep were nervous and answered his questions as forthrightly as they could. For reasons they didn't understand, most of the queries focused on the last stage to change teams here two days earlier. Silleck didn't explain his interest, yet took careful note of their responses.

The locals chose their words carefully and studied him warily. He spoke with a soft Southern drawl, he moved like a cat and his eyes held a dark wild shine.

When he quit they breathed a sigh of relief and traipsed across to the windows to watch him swing astride the mustang with the wind trying to blow his hat off, saw the way he seemed to be smiling to himself as he vanished down the rode for Mile High Plateau.

At first light that morning he'd stood over what the buzzards had left of the body of fellow outlaw Joe Wade. Wade hadn't been a friend; Silleck didn't run to friends. But they'd ridden together for a time before a stranger with two deadly Colts had jumped the bunch at the hole in the wall, and Wade had come out the big loser.

One second-rate gunpacker could be replaced easily enough. That wasn't important. What signified was that someone had been smart enough and interested enough to trail them a far piece before eventually catching up with them. A someone who handled the irons like a pro.

The trail topped out the long climb and the light draining from the sky was reflected in the mustang's mean eye as they crossed the plateau.

From the far north drifted the ghostly whistle of a westbound train tackling the long gradient up to the Dogwood Hills, a relatively new sound for the county if not for Silleck. He'd been places most folks here had never even heard of, just him and his guns and his tetchy black cayuse. He was a loner who was often sought out for special jobs; sometimes, like now, such jobs found him working with others. He didn't mind that, providing they were top gunhands. Wade hadn't been up to scratch and was feeding the buzzards as a result.

The man who'd killed Wade had been a pro. Silleck was sure of it. Sometimes in his bloody work, he would call out and duel another pro on level terms, simply to prove he was the best. Most times he just backshot them and got it over with. Depended on his mood, and he was a moody, murderous man currently engaged on the highest paying contract of his life.

Confidence was this killer's trademark, yet this could be eroded when he was uncertain about exactly who or what he might be up against. Like now.

He turned and shot a glance back over his shoulder as though suddenly expecting to see Wade's killer closing in from behind.

Nothing behind but his own dust.

He swore at his own foolishness and dug the horse cruelly with spur, causing it to jump.

But as full dark came down and the miles flowed behind, his mood altered and assurance returned. Winter was on the march across the Dogwood Hills and he responded to the coming dramas of raging blizzards and mother-murdering avalanches that could engulf you out of the darkness, or simply test out all a man's skills for survival.

Long before raising the lights of the town he was again wearing a cat smile of total confidence, assured in his mind that now they would tag Wade's killer before he tagged them. When that happened, he knew he would choose simply to face the bastard, man to man, and blow him apart just as easily as all the others.

He was a small and supple man whose step was light and quick, yet he was also a giant, for who was bigger than the man who could beat you with a gun on the fastest day you ever lived?

This was the familiar kind of self-worship he often indulged in, and always responded to. The exhilaration it induced was with him all the way until he found himself entering Wagon Street. Then he brought himself down off his high and went and searched for Dimitri.

Duke strolled into the casino room of the Silver Palace from the near-empty theater annex where people were busy erecting scenery and props on the stage. They were yet to light the big chandelier hanging over the faro layout. The skeleton-faced piano professor sat motionless on his three-legged stool, staring at nothing.

The long bar on Duke's right, named the Miner's Retreat, was lined with men's backs. He spared them barely a glance. For these were miners, hairy, hardy brutes only interested in swilling as much beer as they could get down before they puked and staggered off to an early bed. They didn't gamble too heavily, figuring the games were rigged, which they mostly were, most places. But the high-rollers who would show later all reckoned themselves smarter than the house, and some of the top ones really were.

He should know. He was a high roller himself – in his off-duty time.

His work was dangerous and often deadly, and when he relaxed he still gave it everything he had. He was fashioned that way and doubted he would ever change, unless he either stopped the one that mattered, or else struck it rich.

Danger and money might be his only true loves even if at times he might try to fool himself this wasn't so.

The case-keeper perched atop his high stool brooded over his kingdom of bars, carpets, tables, wheels and horseshoe-shaped blackjack layouts from beneath a black eyeshade. The man nodded to Montana and he saluted, feeling relaxed and at home in one of the finest rooms he'd seen outside the big cities.

He sat at an empty table close by the showroom archway and raised two fingers to the black bartender with the huge white smile.

A deck of cards lay on the table. He shuffled them, dealt a couple of hands, considered the result. His two fingers of Godfather's arrived and he leaned back to sip it, dealing another hand one-handed.

Tonight was the sort of night when he would really like to cut loose. His favoured game was blackjack and there were nights when he just knew he would win and there was no way he could lose; nights when the magic flowed from his brain to fingertips and he could tell, nine times out of ten, exactly when the dealer would fold – and Duke Montana would beat the house – again.

But this was also a working night for him, and when a couple of sports sauntered by, he called them over and produced his photograph in its soft leather picture-wallet.

'Seen this girl, fellas? Old friend of mine I'm looking for. Name's Hannah North.'

The men studied the picture. It showed a handsome, dark-haired young woman with wide, serious eyes and full lips. One man whistled softly, both shook their heads.

'Sorry, stranger.'

'You sure?' he prompted. 'I'm half-way certain she's here in Hellfire, or maybe someplace close by.'

'If a looker like that was within fifty miles, we'd know about her,' boasted the second man, and they headed off to the bar, leaving him frowning.

'She's got to be here . . .' he muttered, then looked up as a shadow fell across the table.

'Solitaire?' smirked Ramont. 'Bit of a comedown for the high-roller, ain't it?'

Duke leaned back in his padded chair. Ramont sported evening clothes with a natty black bow tie. The man looked sleek, well-groomed and almost impressive. And, of course, unfriendly. No prize for guessing why.

'Take a card,' Duke drawled. 'Any card. Then I'll draw one blind to beat it.'

The man leaned big-knuckled fists on the table.

'You really are something, ain't you, dude? Big player, big man with the women – even got the law worrying who you are and what game you're playing. Well all that don't cut any ice with me. You don't shape up as anything special in my books.'

Duke began sorting the cards by suit and number.

'So, how is Bella today, anyway?'

The man flushed hotly, straightened.

'Who's talkin' about Bella?'

'You are. All this biggety talk just gives you away. What you're telling me is she's yours and you want me to stay clear. Why don't you just come out with it?'

'All right. Consider it said. She came to this burg with me and she stays with me. Right?'

Duke cut, shuffled, recut, frowned at the result.

'I said – right?'

The man was starting to rile him. Deep down, Duke knew why. Sure, he and Bella were all through. But there were still memories.

He changed the subject. 'You strike me as someone who'd get the lie of a new townplace pretty smart, fella,' he said, eyes on the cards. 'You strike anyone named Dimitri?'

'Same old Montana,' a familiar voice said at his elbow. Bella had come through from the showroom. She always looked good; tonight she looked great in a form-fitting white-silk evening gown and a jewelled band holding her hair snug. She leaned gracefully on the back of his chair and arched an eyebrow. 'You two getting along?'

'Claims he's looking for someone,' Ramont said sourly. 'What was the name?'

Before he could reply, Bella said, 'Still looking for people and asking strange questions, are we, Duke? But of course nobody is ever to know what it's all about,' she added with a touch of bitterness. 'Funny, we knew each other so well, but I never did find out what you did for a living, did I?'

'There was good reason for that, Bella.'

'I'm sure.' Bella cocked her head as the showroom piano began to tinkle. She extended a hand to Ramont. 'Chett's just arrived, Buck. Come along, let's strut our stuff. And remember, we need this job to finance our real job . . . sugar.'

Watching the couple weave their way through the tables for the stage where a woman in a beaded gown sat at a small piano with the saloonkeeper leaning against it, Duke sensed what was coming. Bella was a high-class singer and dancer, when not engaged in some offbeat business scheme or another. But somehow he hadn't figured her new boyfriend as any kind of performer.

How wrong he was.

In the minutes following he and most of the bar crowd watched fascinated as the man in black and the lithe woman in pure white went through an intricate dance routine which showed such polish and style that when it was over, all too quickly, the place erupted into spontaneous applause with even hard-to-please Chett Wilson joining in.

By the time Bella and Ramont returned to the casino they had secured the job they were after, namely appearing twice nightly in the stage shows the Silver Palace put on free to keep the drunks entertained and buying beer.

'Congratulations,' Duke commented. 'Hard work, though.'

'It will pay enough to enable us to get our business

going,' Bella replied, perching on the table as Ramont lighted her cigarette. She inhaled and flashed him a look. 'You see, we came to Hellfire on a mission, Duke.' Her gesture encompassed the crowd. 'Buck has some grounding in the law, and knows a lot about geology and assaying. We're setting up an office where the miners can come and have assays arranged and claims filed and processed and all the rest before the bloodsuckers and parasites get a chance to take them down. Dull but honest work. I'll bet that's something you never expected from me.'

She was dead right about that. Bella could entertain, deal faro, stage-manage a show or charm just about anybody to do just about anything, but 'dull and honest' work was hardly her forte. But in truth he wasn't paying much attention to what she was saying. Watching her dance, step, ripple and sway up there on that little stage in Ramont's arms had stirred some old familiar feelings and, as he got to his feet, Duke Montana wasn't concerned about miners' rights, opportunities, or even the prime reason he'd come here with his photograph tonight.

'Let's dance,' he suggested, extending a hand. 'We always danced pretty fine too, as I recall.'

'Oh, I'm sorry, Duke,' she smiled. 'But here comes Calico.'

'Calico?'

'Yessir, that's me,' grinned the hairy little apelike man with big gnarled hands and grimy coveralls of miner's blue. 'Ready, Miss Bella?'

'I promised Calico first dance earlier,' she

explained, and Duke felt his jaw sag as he watched them move away hand in hand. They found some space, where Calico encompassed her waist with hands as hairy as warthogs, and they began to dance.

'Tough luck,' a voice said at his elbow. Ramont smirked at his discomfiture. 'This is a new Bella, dude. She's given up the old ways. We're going to make a power of difference here for the Cousin Jacks. That's our mission.'

That was the second time Duke had heard that word in five minutes. It was one time too many, and it set him thinking. Bella wasn't exactly a crook, but she loved money more than anyone he'd ever known. He wasn't being superior or judgemental here for he was cut from that same cloth himself. Both had made big bucks and blown them together in those high, heady days in Kansas City. He could hardly be surprised if it was the same lure that Bella was following here as she'd done in Kansas City.

Good luck to her.

But he wasn't swallowing this 'mission' line.

He realized the dancers were attracting an audience. It was Beauty and the Beast on the Silver Palace's polished dance-floor, and the great unwashed were loving it. Bella was so expert she almost succeeded in making Calico look half-way human and less like a bull moose togged out in miner's denim and molly-docker workboots as they made their way around the dance-floor.

Then the light went on in his head.

Of course!

Miners. Gold. Claims. Opportunities.

Present temptations like that in front of a woman like Bella and a streetwise hustler like Ramont, and what did you get?

It was suddenly crystal-clear.

His former lover and her 'dancing partner' hadn't headed for the boondocks simply to help simple prospectors cope with the bloodsuckers and parasites. They were here to slick-trick those poor bums out of their last speck of gold dust. And with Bella running the show, he knew they could do it.

Maybe a man in his line of work should feel offended, but he wasn't. He was a realist. Life was hard by the yard and anything but a cinch by the inch. A man – or woman – did what it took to survive in this tough life.

Montana was rarely judgemental, but he was a man totally dedicated to his job. And quite suddenly he decided it was too early to get too serious about relaxation. His sense of morality, though mighty flexible at times, was still operating. And right now, banishing beautiful Bella from mind, as he knew he must, he headed briskly for the batwings, reminding himself of the seriousness of his assignment and the need to get on with it. Time to stop working at half-pace and get on with the job of flushing out pretty Hannah North before someone else found and murdered her.

The following night fell black. A chill wind blew from the north as the horseman made his careful way through the canyon. White stars blinked into life and a weird moon rose directly ahead to outline grotesque shapes, pillars and tombs and rearing monuments to Nature's dead sculpted by the wind and sand of Hard Luck Canyon.

It had earned its name early in the gold frenzy days when a miner was killed by an avalanche the very day he struck it rich. His ghost was supposed to haunt the place still.

Ghosts didn't bother this rider, and he reckoned mining was for losers anyway. He made his living with the guns, and a .44 was in his hand as his mustang carried him up to the rim and something stirred ahead.

Silleck reined in sharply. 'Dimitri?'

'Who else?'

He covered the last thirty yards and reined in. The man he'd come to meet was a large silhouette on an outsized quarter horse, man and horse looking twelve feet high in the moonlight.

'What's doing?' the statue asked.

'It's the dude. Montana. He's totin' a picture of the woman about, askin' all sorts of questions.'

'Anyone know anything about him?'

'The new singer and dancer at the Silver Palace reckons she knew him down south. But she won't talk about him. I tried her. But I dogged that flash sonuva some today. He's workin' overtime with his lousy photygraph. I even saw him showin' it to the John Law.'

The big figure stiffened. 'That ties it. He's got to go.'

'Er, you want me to—'

'No. We gotta work on findin' her ourselves. I'll

send you a couple of hardcases to take care of the dude. They'll meet you at noon at the Red Ace.'

With that the big man swung his horse and loped off. Silleck lingered long enough to fashion and light a brown-paper quirley. He flicked the dead match away and rode back the way he'd come.

He felt strangely relaxed and peaceful with the tall shelves surrounding him, the quiet of the brick-walled building sinking in. Had he ever been in a library before? He doubted it. But there was some-thing companionable about endless shelves of books by people with names like Tolstoy, Dickens and one even he recognized, William Shakespeare.

'*The Tempest*,' he murmured, and was reaching for the leather-bound volume when the discreet sound of flat-heeled shoes on polished linoleum caused him to drop his hand and turn.

'Can I assist you, sir?'

The librarian appeared to be middle-aged even though her hair, dressed in a severe style and drawn back in a tight bun, was completely gray. Horn-rimmed spectacles, ill-fitting tweed suit and a stern expression completed the impression of a no-nonsense female who took herself and life with total seriousness.

He hazarded a half-hearted smile. No reaction. Not much hope of impressing this one, Montana. He had a feeling she was staring right through him with those big mannish spectacles and thinking: *He must have wandered in by mistake . . . probably searching for a bookmaker, not a book repository. . . .*

He sobered and said, 'It seems you don't have what I'm looking for, Mrs . . . ?'

'Jones. And just what might you be interested in, Mr . . . ?

'Duke Montana. It's an obscure book and I can't recall the name. But just so my visit isn't a total waste of time, dear lady, would you mind taking a look at this?'

He'd produced his little photo-wallet so often over the past two days he reckoned he could do it in his sleep.

'This is a young woman I've been searching for, a Miss Hannah North, late of Capital City. You must have a hell of a lot of people go through here, Mrs Jones. Have you seen her?'

Squinting and frowning the woman studied the photograph for some time before shaking her head.

'I'm sorry, but I've never seen this person before. And I have a good memory for faces.' She sniffed and studied him over the rim of the glasses. 'Might I enquire the reason for your interest in this Miss North, Mr Montana?'

He sighed as he slipped the wallet away.

'Missing person, family grieving. You know. The old story. Well, thank you for your time, ma'am.' He turned to go, then paused. 'Was there something?'

'No. Why?'

'For a second I thought you were about to say something more.'

She shook her head firmly, as sober as a mother superior.

'Sorry, you were mistaken.'

He fitted his hat to his head, nodded, and quit the big echoing room to walk out into a gray day that wasn't improved any when he saw the sheriff leaning an elbow on the stone balustrade.

'Sheriff.' His tone was guarded. Conway Dunstan didn't like his kind, and it showed. 'Taking a breather?'

'No, I've been waiting to see you.' Dunstan rested fists on hips, blocking his way down the steps. 'Tell me again, mister. How was it you came to flag down the last stage at Mulroney's Creek with nothing but what you stood up in?'

'I already told you.'

'Tell me again.'

'My horse bolted and I was left afoot. Simple.'

'Ever been to Prairie Valley?'

Warning bells chimed. He felt the need of a cheroot but decided against lighting up. Instead he folded his arms and looked bored.

'Never even heard of it.'

'Now that's odd. It's only four or five miles from where they picked you up.'

'Make your point, Sheriff. I can tell you've got one.'

The lawman leaned forward challengingly. 'They found a decomposing body down the valley this morning. Man about thirty, shot dead maybe three-four days ago. Could have been the same day the stage picked you up down there, to hell and gone from anyplace. Seems to me you might have seen something, heard something . . . know something. Well?'

'What I know is that you are hinting I could have

47

had something to do with that killing.'

'You were in the vicinity.'

'So were they.'

'Who?'

'Six drovers and forty head of cattle. Circle D. They came up through the valley that same day, heading for Mulroney's Creek. They all suspects too?'

The lawman flushed. He was playing a long shot and it had backfired on him. He knew about the cattle drive, hadn't expected Duke to know also.

Their stares locked and held for a long moment before Dunstan swore softly and moved aside, allowing him to step past. Then he called:

'What were you doing at the library?'

Duke halted. 'You know what. Showing my picture.'

'That female's not here, never been here. I told you that.'

'I've a hunch she is here.'

'And I'm telling you—'

'No,' Duke cut in, 'I'm telling you, Dunstan. I came to your town searching for a missing person and you've given me no help at all. That's fine. What's not fine is you not even trying to help out, just giving me trouble. Maybe you should back off.'

The lawman paled. 'Are you threatening me?'

'Call it what you like,' Duke snapped, turning away. 'But it just could be you're way out of your depth, tinstar.'

Red-faced and angry, the sheriff took two long steps after him. Montana glanced back and something in his eyes caused Dunstan to prop. Something deadly.

'Damned dude gunslicks!' he muttered, but Duke didn't hear. He lengthened his stride as he made his way along the plankwalk, figuring where he'd stop off next. Time was running short and he was being pressed for results from above. The people he worked for were experts at many things, including applying pressure.

Silleck stepped outside the rough plank-and-batten bar where the sun held a little warmth, where life was moving sluggishly through Hellfire late in the afternoon. Three women in austere quakercloth and sober straw hats emerged from the doctor's chambers three doors along, then pointedly crossed the street upon sighting him standing there with his elbows on the hitch rail and an unlit cigarette pasted to the corner of his mouth.

He grinned and winked when one peeked back over her shoulder. Hellfire had a sub-culture of nameless, idle drifters and bums, and fine upstanding ladyfolks had every reason to avoid them. They thought he was shiftless, and were dead right about that. Shiftless, dangerous and, on this afternoon, just a little edgy. Fate was upping the stakes in the game he was involved in. There had been no gunplay or bloodshed since he'd shown up in Hellfire ten days earlier, but that was about to change.

He lighted his cigarette, smoked it through and was turning to head for the Indian Queen when he sighted them turning into St Leque Street from the corner of his eye.

Two riders.

He stood motionless as they drew nearer, threading their way through the late afternoon traffic. They were nondescript men, wearing floppy black hats and enveloped in travel-stained gray dusters that concealed any guns they might be carrying. Bearded faces were blank and the pair seemed focused on the way ahead. Yet as they drew level the nearer rider turned his head and dropped him a wink.

Silleck felt his pulse lift its beat. They had come, just as Dimitri had said they would. The killers. He felt a tingling in his wrists and straightaway started in planning how he would set himself up with a rock-solid alibi to have ready for later tonight when the gunners went to work.

He stopped for a quick one at the Golden Nugget and it was coming on dark when he emerged, the lamplighter just completing his rounds in his flat-bed wagon.

He paused on sighting a familiar figure on the opposite walk. As usual, Montana was striding along as though he owned the place as he made for the Silver Palace like a starving man who'd just heard the dinner gong. But tonight there was something different concerning this man whom he'd been warned to keep clear of. Montana was being tagged, or at least it appeared that way to him, who knew a thing or two about the art of following people.

As he stopped on the edge of the planking to stare, the dowdy figure well in back of Montana's tall silhouette moved through a slab of light spilling from the doorway of Goodpasture's Emporium. He scratched the back of his head on recognizing the frumpy female from the library, just one of the dozens of women they'd checked out early in their search for a woman named Hannah North, the same missing person Duke the dude Montana was looking for.

He grinned at a thought. Hey, maybe flash Montana had done Miss Hornrims wrong, and now she was after him with a butcher's knife tucked in her drawers.

The grin slowly faded and he was sober again. No. Nobody but the brothers would be entrusted with that job which they'd been paid to do. Yet he found himself wishing it was already over and done. The moment he first clapped eyes on Duke Montana, this expert in such matters had assessed him as a hard man to kill.

But one way or another, the dude must die.

CHAPTER 4

COLD CARDS, HOT LEAD

Duke was winning serious money.

Duke was just in front, but not by much.

Duke was not in front at all. But with the casino clock chiming 1 a.m. he was reluctantly forced to think about tomorrow.

'In or out, old buddy?' grinned the boss of the Lady Clara Mine, who was in front by a country mile. Montana was popular at the Palace as a fearless gambler and great company. Sometimes drinkers ringed the poker layout just to watch 'the Duke' when he was riding a streak, but there was no audience tonight as his luck appeared to have disappeared down all drains.

He studied his fellow-players, the mine boss, three of his engineers, a visiting banker from Capital City and a bob-wire salesman from Minnesota. And his cocky self said, *You should be able to beat a bunch like this both blindfold and drunk.*

So, why was he losing?

He was sure he was reading this lousy poker-game right, knew he could reverse his fortunes in just two or three more hands. Even so, he now found himself shoving his chair back from the table and cussing Dixie as he got to his feet.

If the perky percenter hadn't made such a big play for him, and if he had only reminded himself it wasn't really obligatory for him to play just as hard as he worked every night of the week – instead of disappearing upstairs with her for two hours – he felt rock-solid certain he'd be walking away from this high-stake game of poker the big winner.

If only.

OK, so he'd had a fine time, as indeed had been the case every night he'd been in this town. A man had to relax and the pattern of his life now, for longer than he wanted to remember, had been to cram just as much into having one hell of a good time as he invested in his work.

Yet he sensed strongly that something other than romance had motivated him to climb the wide stairs with pretty Dixie on his arm – precisely and deliberately at the moment Bella and Ramont swept onstage to perform for the paying customers who packed out the showroom every night solid.

He'd made damn sure Bella saw them.

But she'd gotten square at the conclusion of their late show when she'd kissed that tap-dancing gigolo full on the lips for about ten seconds – strictly for his benefit, he knew. The audience, mostly miners, had applauded wildly. She was already their golden dream girl. He was aware that she and Ramont had set up their business and were already handling a fair amount of miners' claims and suchlike from their shonky little office on Wagon Street. The diggers would likely get taken for a ride, but that was no concern of his – any more than she was. . . .

But fitting his hat to his head and checking himself out in the back-bar mirror, he stopped scowling and looked on the positive side. He couldn't argue but that Dixie – all the way from the deep South – had certainly taken his mind off his lack of progress in his assignment for yet another day, and that had to be a big plus.

'Had enough?' asked a familiar voice.

Chett Wilson sat by the faro layout near the exit nursing a chorus girl and a building hangover. The saloonkeeper liked Montana and admired his swashbuckling style, but still wanted him gone. He sensed some powerful connection between the Duke and the Palace's new star attraction, and Wilson didn't want to see this man stirring up anything that might divert Bella from her work, or worse, cause her to up and quit.

Duke's smile was amiable.

'That'll be the day. I'll be back to take it all back plus another few hundred tomorrow night.'

'That's how I get rich, mister. Confident suckers. Ain't that so, Jilly?'

'I'm Cissy,' murmured the sleepy girl. She dropped a smoky wink at Duke. 'And he's cute. Aren't you, cutie? I know Bella reckons so.'

54

Wilson bucked her off his knee and got to his feet.

'You know nothing, baby,' he snapped, waving her off. He turned back to Duke and forced a grin. He might be drunk but he was still the canny business-man. 'Montana, you seem a smart enough sort of fella. And you like money, I've seen that. Just between you and me, what would it take for you to, you know, climb aboard a horse or a train and just vanish?'

Suddenly Duke was weary. Wilson was as easy to read as a kid's primer.

'Relax, man,' he said, turning to go. 'I'm here on business and Bella isn't it. She can dance for your Cousin Jacks with her gigolo until she's too old to get up on the stage. Me? I've got work to do.'

'I'd like to believe you, but the truth is I feel there's something about you that just doesn't ring true, pard. Guy like you pounding the pavements looking for runners? What sort of money's in that? Peanuts. C'mon, name your price to get lost and let Bella settle down all happy and peaceful. Two hundred? Three? Hey! Where you going?'

But Montana was already gone. And by the time he'd pushed through the batwings, tipped the big black doorman, and stepped out into the cold street he'd put both Wilson and his drunken offer from his mind. For what he'd said was true. He did have work to do. And Bella didn't mean anything to him anymore. Well, scarcely anything.

He headed for the hotel. The wide street was almost deserted now, although Benny the Bum was still abroad and on the cadge.

'Clean 'em out again tonight, Mr Duke?' He grinned, shivering in his thin coat with the frayed sleeves. For some reason Montana always attracted people like this, who found him a soft touch. 'I reckon you're the hottest danged player they've ever see at the Palace . . .'

He broke off as Duke flipped him a silver dollar but waved away the profuse thanks, quickening his stride as he headed for the Union Street corner.

Funny thing, but a man never seemed to go home tired when he'd won.

The darkened store-fronts reflected the yellow glare of the street lamps, and his image appeared in some of them, distorted and jerky. He was idly imagining what it would feel like actually to be five feet wide by five high, when he paused with a sudden frown.

Somewhere in back of him, also mirrored by the distorting windows of the assay office, was a vaguely familiar figure following him. Turning, he saw it was a woman shrouded in a shapeless greatcoat with a scarf tied round her head.

He stopped and she stopped. She seemed scared, as any woman abroad alone in a mining town at this hour would have good reason to be.

Hesitantly, the woman reached up to brush a strand of hair from her brow, and recognition hit. The attendant from the library.

She made as if to hurry off, but he beckoned and said:

'It's OK, Mrs Jones. You looking for me?'

She didn't respond, but didn't take flight either.

He strolled back slowly as to not startle her. He fingered his hat back off his face, thinking: Always be wary when someone acts out of character. Bureau regulations. They had a million of them.

'Ma'am?' he said, drawing up.

He expected her to be scared when he drew close, but that wasn't the case. Her shoulders were damp, indicating she'd been outdoors for some time. The gray hair was straggly. Yet her look was direct and her voice firm enough when she eventually spoke.

'I needed to see you tonight, Mr Montana. I've been waiting for you to leave the saloon.'

He made a gesture. 'We can talk at my hotel. Warmer.'

'No, thank you. This won't take but a moment. I've come to ask something very special of you, young man. I . . . I want you to give up this search for the woman you are looking for. Miss North. Not only that, but I'd very much appreciate it if you would consider leaving Hellfire.'

He ginned.

'Seems lots of folk would like me to go, ma'am. But I've got to say I'm not always this unpopular—'

'I'm quite serious,' she cut in, drawing a little closer. 'You see, I can't explain all my reasons for my request. But I do happen to believe that your coming here and making all these enquiries about Miss North could be putting her life at great risk.'

Now he was the serious one.

'You know where she is?' he asked sharply.

'No, of course not. But can't you see? If this unhappy young woman was hiding somewhere in this region, she must have the best of reasons, and she could only feel terribly threatened by someone like you arriving from nowhere and raising a great fuss about her, even offering a reward for information concerning her whereabouts.'

'You do know something . . .'

He broke off as the woman stifled a sob, turned abruptly, and ran. He started after her, then halted. She moved quite fast for a woman her age. She was obviously in a highly emotional state. He wondered if she might be in possession of some information or knowledge of the missing woman, otherwise, why the desperate plea?

Waiting until she vanished, he turned slowly to retrace his steps, massaging the back of his neck. Of course she had a point, he conceded. There was implicit risk in his anything-but-private search. This was regrettable yet unavoidable. Were he free to do so, he could have revealed to Mrs Jones that certain powerful and ruthless people were also acutely interested in locating Hannah North, which paradoxically was one of the reasons his masters had chosen him to locate her with all possible speed. He was considered a swift and reliable operator with skills at dealing with women – too many skills, some in Capital City might argue.

He knew he would be at the library at nine o'clock, whether it upset Mrs Jones or not. This could literally be a matter of life or death.

He was relieved when he tramped up Union Street and saw the hotel welcoming him in the dim street-light, its gables and shadowed galleries welcoming at the fag-end of a long, mixed day.

The owl flew purposefully in from the dark woods which crowded the back lots beyond Jessie Street, reaching Union with heavy wingbeats then gliding the remaining fifty yards, plainly intending to land atop the hotel around which bats were to be found late at night.

He was barely aware of the predator until it emitted a sharp hoot of alarm. Within some fifty feet of the roof, which was blocked from Duke's vision at this angle by the façade, the bird abruptly veered away sharply with another hoot and flew on swiftly to vanish behind the giant maple in back of the hotel stables.

Duke stood totally motionless. But now he had a gun in his hand.

Stripped of boots, jacket and hat, Montana went up the outside fire-escape in total silence, every sense taut, sixguns at waist level and ready for instant use.

Sure, it could be something totally harmless that had scared the bird. A prowling cat, a sudden movement at a window. But when a man lived with danger he learned early and learned good; never take anything for granted and always expect the worst until proven otherwise.

He reached the top floor without incident. The Territory Hotel seemed locked in dignified silence. The gable roof thrust sharply overhead. There was a sturdy railing, and he mounted it then slowly straightened until pausing with his head at gutter-height.

He listened.

Nothing. No bats, birds or night crawlers. Impulse wanted him to rise that extra foot and take a peek; training and experience said the opposite. Being sure wasn't enough. You had to be dead sure.

Seconds ticked by and he'd about decided caution had been satisfied when it came to him as clearly to his straining ears as the clamor of an alarm bell. Someone had cleared their throat, a soft, suppressed sound that saw him gently, noiselessly cock both .45s before moving.

He straightened.

A wide expanse of moon-silvered roof slanting away from a row of room windows, of which his own was one. Hard by his sill, sprawled out flat and facing the window with light flaring along the barrel of the revolver in his fist, was a big man, wearing a gray duster. Ten feet further on, also intent upon his room window, was a second man, armed and attired like the first, now turning his shaggy heady to stare in his direction, then jolt with shock.

Montana's Colts were resting on the metal guttering.

'Freeze, you sons of bitches!'

The dustcoats bucked like startled beasts and the moment their guns jerked his way he knew what he had to do.

His first bullet struck the closer man's gun arm, bringing a choked-off cry of pure agony. He swung his smoking cutter on the second man but was forced to duck before he could trigger as gunflame gushed orange and wicked and something snorted past his

60

left ear like a hornet.

With gun echoes reverberating all about him, and the first man retrieving his dropped gun with his left hand, Montana wasn't aiming to take prisoners or simply defend himself any longer. These bastards were out to kill him – big surprise! The uninjured man was the faster of the two. He was a heavyweight with a snarling, sweating face who blinked involuntarily as he jerked trigger.

With a cold hard knot in his gut, Montana watched the muzzle spit boreflame. He imagined he felt the hot breath of the explosion in his face. He ducked rattlesnake fast and the bullet gouged the guttering where he'd been an instant before, ricocheting with a banshee wail.

There was lethal purpose in his every movement as he whipped a gun over the rim. Somewhere close by a woman began shrieking, there was the sound of glass breaking as someone fumbled for a light. The Colt was solid and heavy in Montana's hand. He triggered without needing to aim, knowing if he missed at this range he was in the wrong business.

He fired and missed.

Leastways he missed his intended target as the closer man, leaking blood and his black gun in his left hand, jerked upwards with the intention of firing at him at point blank range.

Montana's slug caught him between the eyes and spattered his brains over the man behind him.

Dead already, the dry-gulcher seemed to take forever to slump. Long enough for his horrified henchman to drop his gun and begin beating hysterically at the gray matter covering his, face and upper body, forgetting he was on a steeply sloping roof.

He howled as he went over the rim, branches ripping loose as his fall was broken by a nearby tree, all the while screaming like a woman.

Montana went after him.

There were two ways the dustcoat could go when he hit ground, left or right along the rear wall of the hotel. Montana chose the right, sped to the corner, realized he'd guessed wrong, started back.

He heard the sounds of a horse starting up just as he made it to the corner. Half-hidden by foliage, the gray figure hugged his horse's neck as it went leaping away. Snarling, cursing, Montana emptied one revolver futilely but allowed the second gun to hang when he realized his quarry was gone.

He leaned against the corner and sleeved his forehead as lights began blooming in the windows above. In the wake of the gunplay the startled, hysterical voices seemed muted and childlike to his ears.

Slowly he holstered and retraced his steps to the fire escape to find out who he'd just killed. And await the arrival of the law.

'Not good enough, mister,' Dunstan snapped, and it was hard to believe he wasn't enjoying this. 'Two men, so you say, tried to kill you. Yet you admit you never saw either in your life, can't think of a single motive why perfect strangers might want you dead. Two men were allegedly waiting on your return to your hotel, yet you – a saloon lizard and cardsharp by trade as far as I can figure – you got the drop on them, killed one stone dead and his partner conveniently disappears. I have got your story right, haven't I?'

Fully dressed now but for his hat, Duke Montana inhaled a lungful of soothing cigar smoke and flicked ash into the brass desk-tray.

He appeared the calmest man in town, likely was. Murderous sixgun duels of the kind that had jolted every single one of Hellfire's two thousand plus citizens wide awake in the early hours of the morning were anything but new to this self-described 'searcher of missing persons'.

He wasn't indifferent to the fact that a man had died but he wasn't fretting any either. He'd have pegged both out to dry had he been quick enough, and counted the moment sweet.

He blew a perfect smoke-ring and said:

'Two strangers jumped me, I killed one, the other escaped. End of story. Now if there's nothing else I—'

'You'll what?' Conway Dunstan was mostly a level-headed kind of peace officer, no headliner, but reliable and a stickler for the letter of the law. But because he sensed his town slipping away from him, with strangers and hardcases seeming to proliferate by the day, he was ready to take a stand. And who better to make an example of than a man whose appearance, manner, lifestyle and general flashy popularity on the streets, especially with the womenfolk, was so much his polar opposite?

Besides, the sheriff genuinely felt there was something suspicious about the shoot-out and wasn't about to permit the prime protagonist simply to put on his hat and stroll out into the night, where he would be just as likely to vanish for ever, if he was any judge.

Dramatically, or so it seemed to Montana, the man reached for his key-ring hanging from an iron wall-bracket.

'What?' Duke's black brows arched high.

'Sorry about this, Montana, but under the circumstances I don't have any option but to hold you until the morning, when I can conduct a proper investigation.'

Montana didn't move yet seemed to change before the lawman's eyes. No hint of an easy smile now, none of the charm that was responsible for his being so popular here. This Montana, still not moving or speaking, suddenly looked about as dangerous a man as Conway Dunstan had ever faced.

The lawman jingled his keys and cleared his throat.

'Cells are pretty comfortable, young fella. You can have number two, it's got—'

'Forget it.' Montana was on his feet in one rippling motion. He didn't move any closer to the sheriff, yet Dunstan felt compelled to take a step backwards. Duke rested hands on hips, brushing back the panels of his coat to reveal the unspoken challenge of polished sixgun handles and glinting cartridge rims. 'I've played it straight with you, Dunstan, even though you took a notion to dislike me the day I rode in. That's your right. But it's my right – when a man who ought know better starts acting like a jackass – to remind him of that fact and give him a sporting chance to back water before he pushes something so far there's no going back.'

Dunstan's mouth was dry. Outside, the deputies were talking with the small crowd that had gathered in the aftermath of the excitement. The man watched Montana draw on his cheroot, felt a nerve begin to tic in his cheek.

'You're under arrest,' he insisted, sounding like a man who had no place to go but ahead now. 'I'll have your weapons, mister.'

Montana put a lazy circle of smoke between them.

The desk clock ticked too loudly.

Beads of cold sweat stood out on Dunstan's head. Then he yelled:

'Boys! Get in here, we got a problem.'

Montana's guns filled his hands in a motion that appeared lazy and relaxed, but wasn't. Ashen-faced, Dunstan backed towards his desk as the door swung open and the taller deputy led his stockier companion into the front office. The pair stopped on a dime when they saw the naked guns.

'What the tarna—?' said the first man.

'I won't explain,' Montana drawled, circling them to make for the door. He flicked a muzzle in Dunstan's direction. 'I came here to do a job of work that's more important than you could ever imagine, mister. So important, in truth, that I mean to go on doing it just like before tonight's dust-up. I won't be breaking any laws, I won't give you tinstars any trouble. But if you try to stop me doing my work then you're going to have to ask yourselves: Is it worth it? Is it worth tangling with a man you know to be innocent – and who's had more gunfights than you've had hot meals. Think that one over before you come down with any loco notion, such as following me.'

He had three frozen men standing before him. The lawmen weren't cowards, but they weren't fools either.

'You won't get away with this,' was the best Dunstan could come up with.

Montana just nodded, and was easing towards the door when it swung inwards and a man strode in as though he owned the place. He was tall with a military bearing and clipped mustache.

'Just as I expected, Montana,' he stated acerbically. 'Why is it that my instincts never fail me where you are concerned, unhappily.' He swung to face the sheriff who was reaching his carbine down from the wall. 'All right, Sheriff, my name is Polk, I know this gentleman and I've heard what happened tonight. What, as they say at Lords, is the state of play?'

Dunstan stared. He was white-faced and angry.

'Damn you, mister,' he said angrily, 'what gives you the right to come storming into my jailhouse acting like you're some kind of—'

'This does.'

The man called Polk had taken a wallet from an inner pocket, which he held at arm's length before Dunstan's eyes. The lawman scanned the card he presented, read it again, looked up wide-eyed.

Polk insisted the lawmen check out several documents.

'These establish that I am really the card-holder,

66

sir. I trust you find these in order?'

Dunstan set his carbine on the desk, riffled through the documents, finally nodded and returned them.

'I . . . I guess you are who and what you say, Mr Polk. But this flash gun-tipper here is—'

'Is a fellow employee of the same organization identified on my card,' Polk stated impatiently. 'What are the charges?'

Dunstan glanced at Montana, who hadn't spoken since Polk's arrival. He appeared bored and unsurprised by this development as he adjusted his string tie by a small square of mirror on the wall.

'Pay attention, Montana,' Polk snapped. 'As this matter intimately concerns you.'

Montana completed what he was doing before catching Polk's eye in the glass.

'Don't tell me what to do, Polk.' He spoke softly but he was sore. The shoot-out, Dunstan's reaction and now the appearance of this man, who was indeed his superior, was a combination that affected him adversely. Then he turned and said to Dunstan, 'There aren't any charges, are there, Sheriff? Of course, if there are, they'll be contested and you'll be the loser.'

He cut a steely gaze at a glowering Polk. 'Ready to go – as they say at Lords?'

He sauntered out and the tall man followed, mustache bristling.

'No!' a slumping Dunstan said as his deputies began firing questions. 'Not now. Later . . . maybe. Smitty, take this fool rifle away and pour me a drink.'

'But . . . but you never drink on duty, Sheriff.'
'Don't argue man. Pour!'

CHAPTER 5

DOING IT TOUGH

Lights showed up ahead as Silleck pushed his wild-eyed mustang round the corner in the trail where a titanic white pine reached for the stars.

The doors of the Whiskey Shack Trailhouse never closed. It stood on the OK Trail ten miles north of Hellfire on a lonesome stretch of deeply rutted road, but the Dogwood Hills diggings sprawled across the hilltops less than five miles distant. They worked shifts at places like the Sister Fan and Viking mines, and diggers, drillers, muleskinners and lamp-boys always needed someplace to get a drink after the quit bell rang.

The hardcase shivered as a mean wind snaked out of the tall timbers and tossed the horse's coal-black mane. Silleck was a man who liked his comfort, would still be snug in bed but for what had happened overnight.

He sighted two tethered horses, a long-legged bay and a nondescript gray mare as he drew closer to the lights. He nodded. Dimitri and Brodie were here already; no sign of August's big stallion as yet.

He touched up the black to come in neat, tied up to the battered old hitch rail. The doors were propped open and he could hear drunken voices raised in song as he climbed the steps with his light, lithe step. Miners. Some never got further than the Shack with their paycheck. The trailhouse keeper would likely die rich from their custom, which was more than most of them could ever expect to do.

A sneer flickered along the edges of his mind when he glimpsed the big figure in a weatherstained dustcoat slumped at a table. Brodie looked like a loser. Was. The man would get no sympathy from him. The dustcoat brothers had been given a simple job and botched it. Maybe he should have taken the job himself.

Dimitri grunted a greeting. They had a double shot waiting for him on the table. Silleck fingered his hat back and took a chair, sleek, dark and yellow-eyed in the flickering lamplight.

'So?' he grunted, staring at Brodie.

'You heard?' the man replied.

'Of course I freakin' heard. The whole goddamn county knows by now. What happened?'

'You never told us the dude was a gun wizard,' the bruised and battered Brodie complained. He brushed at his duster front and grimaced. 'Done blew Jury's brains all over me, he did, for God's sake.'

'Yeah, yeah.' Silleck glanced at Dimitri, seated sphynx-like and impassive as always. Looked more Mongol than American even though he was a third

70

generation Carolinian, so he always felt. 'Kurt comin'?'

'Sure.' Dimitri was a man who didn't waste words. Or bullets. He too was sore at Brodie. He and Silleck had hired the brothers for the Montana job. Kurt August wouldn't be happy about the outcome, and who could blame him.

One of the miner quartet from the back room broke away from 'Sweet Adeline' and came lurching by the table, heading for out back. Full of cheap booze and *bonhomie*, he paused to boom an amiable greeting.

'Shut up and get lost, bum!' Silleck snarled. Dimitri backed him up with one of his glacial stares which saw the man flinch and reel away, take fresh bearings, then vanish without another word.

They weren't here for socializing. This was about as serious as it got.

Silleck was working on his second double when they heard a horse draw up outside just as the first faint wisp of gray touched the eastern rim.

Kurt August walked in, peeling off yellow roper's gloves. A man below average height, the former ship's mate was an iron jawed skeleton who dressed neatly but not showily. A man designed by nature to give orders rather than take them, he was the contact between the gunmen and the mystery men financing their activities.

As expected, August was far from pleased by the results of the bloody gundown at the Territory Hotel. But he wasn't a man to gripe or to 'if only'. He heard the story from Brodie's own lips, considered, produced a wad of cash, handed it to the dustcoat, and said quietly:

'Now get lost.'

Brodie reddened. He was genuinely grieving for his brother. If that hadn't been the case he mightn't have done what he did.

'I don't want your stinkin' blood-money!' he raged. And lunging to his feet, he flung the notes in August's face.

Off-balanced, Brodie dropped his hand onto the table top to steady himself. Silleck's gunbutt smashed down upon the splayed fingers and Brodie turned ashen with agony. His moaning cut off when Dimitri rose with curious massive grace, seized him by his dustcoat and flung him fifteen staggering feet towards the doors before he could steady himself.

'Just collect your money, sit down and shut up. Nobody quits.' Silleck's voice was calm and cold. The badman began to weep but did as ordered.

'Been in touch with our boss?' Silleck asked August. The man nodded, and he went on: 'Guess he's pretty sore, huh?'

'You could say that.' August as always was brief and to the point. 'Montana's still got to go. He's a lot more than we figured at first, and he's sticking to the scent like a bluestick hound. We don't know if he's onto the dame. But someone sprang him from the hoosegow a couple hours back, and our guess is that it was whoever that sonuva's working for. We tipped our hand by siccing those two bums after him, so we've got to lie low right now until things settle some.'

He rose with an air of finality.

'Stick with Hellfire, it's still our best bet. Keep watching Montana and keep hunting for the dame, but don't let him know it. That'll do it until I get fresh orders.'

He turned to leave but Silleck halted him.

'What if Montana should flush that bitch afore we see you, Kurt?'

'Whole new set of rules if that happens.' August's clean-shaven Nordic features were without expression. 'Kill him then meet me here.'

'What about her?' Dimitri wanted to know.

August spoke over his shoulder as he walked off.

'Her too. Welcome to the big game, boys.'

The sleepy-eyed housemaid placed the tray on the low cane table in the center of the room: coffee, pancakes, molasses and a side order of fruit for 'Mr Montana's guest'. She glanced at Duke with a mixture of admiration and unease. She'd never seen a man who'd been shot to death until tonight. The girl was amazed that their guest appeared totally unfazed by the affair. He also seemed quite unimpressed by his dignified guest, Mr Polk of Capital City.

Pouring hot black joe for himself, Montana dropped the girl a wink and she left silently, the door whispering shut on her back. Ignoring Polk's critical stare, he carried his cup to the french doors and stared out. It was coming on first light. He'd never been more wide-awake. Nothing like having someone try to kill you and someone else try to throw you in the slammer to sharpen a man up and concentrate his thinking.

They'd sluiced down the roof outside but some stains remained. They were red. Montana took a strong pull on his coffee. You told yourself you didn't give a damn, but a man's inner voice sometimes had other ideas. His could be a real nag at times. He sensed it preparing to chide him for not showing more reaction than he was – was almost relieved when Polk got in first.

'You're working well, Investigator Montana. Chase suspects to Prairie Valley – kill a man. Fail to find your party here in Hellfire – kill another man. Not much in the way of results for our report, I'll grant you. But we can't accuse you of losing your touch in the weaponry department, now can we?'

Duke continued to survey the sleeping houses, the forests beyond, the awakening hills. They'd clashed many a time in the past and he saw no reason why this time should be any different.

Montana's official designation with the organization which employed them both, was field man. Polk's was executive officer in charge of field personnel. Montana was paid more than his superior because field men had short lives due to the nature of their work, and demanded and received salaries commensurate with those risks. Executive officers, on the other hand, could look forward to a safe and secure working life followed by retirement on a handsome pension, goals no field man had ever succeeded in surviving long enough to achieve in the organization's existence.

The organization was called the Bureau.

'How's Cullenmore these days?' he asked idly. He didn't give a damn how the chief might be, but such questions always irked Polk, who lusted after Chief Cullenmore's exalted position.

'I warned them,' Polk went on, as though he'd not interrupted. 'I protested in writing that I regarded Field Man Montana as too unpredictable, excitable, even unstable for such an important assignment. But would they listen? No. Insisted they must have an investigator with an "empathy" for women – for God's sweet sake – and a proven capacity for decisive action when called for. So, what do we have after five weeks? Two corpses, an outraged sheriff and a traumatized town. And, of course, no Hannah North. Remarkably chaotic even by your standards, wouldn't you agree?'

Montana turned.

'Quit blowin' on the fur and git to the hide,' he said with an exaggerated drawl. 'As mah pappy used say. So you showed up at the right time. Nice timing. I'm in your debt. So, what next?'

The man from Capital City perched on the arm of a plush chair and sipped his coffee, little finger crooked.

'I'll recommend your withdrawal from Operation North, of course.'

'Waste of time. I'm Cully's fair-headed boy after the last job – which also claimed I couldn't handle – and we both know it. And to state the obvious, this is a risky job, maybe as risky as I've handled. There are people out there just as determined to find her as we are, and those two dead men is all the proof you need to understand that they are playing for keeps.'

'What progress have you made?'

'It's all in my log.'

He indicated a leather-covered black book on the low table. Polk picked it up, began leafing through. Sniffing. Then something caught his eye. He swung his elongated head sharply.

'Bella Duvall? Is that the same B—'

'Yeah.'

'The one you were cohabiting with in Sun River while you were working on the Big Six assignment? Dancer, confidence trickster, temperamental hellcat and troublemaker? That woman is here in Hellfire . . .' Polk broke off as suspicion hit. He uncoiled to his full six-four. 'You brought her here with you, didn't you? By glory, man, when Cullenmore hears about this—'

'Sorry to disappoint you, but Miss Duvall's being here is pure coincidence.'

'Pure?'

'Don't push your luck, management man,' Duke warned. 'OK, let's get down to cases. I'm working hard on this job and I'm making progress. If you apply to have me taken off the assignment I'll quit and make sure Cully knows why. Further to that, I'm the only field man on the Bureau's books right now who knows this assignment backwards and has got what it takes to see it through. You know it, but you hate my guts. Well, that's OK. It's mutual . . .'

He broke off at a knock on the door. 'Yeah?'

The maid appeared.

'Someone to see you, Mr Duke, sir.'

'At this hour? Better tell them to—'

'A Miss Duvall, sir.'

'Bella? Here?' He frowned in puzzlement. 'I'll be damned. All right, send her up, Cissy.' The door remained open, and he smiled cheerfully at his superior. 'Don't let me keep you.'

But Polk stood his ground.

'This I wouldn't miss for worlds, hotshot.' His manner was sarcastic. 'I'm sure I'm about to be impressed by this paragon of virtue who shared your bed and helped make almost a farce of your Sun River investigation . . .'

He broke off as Bella Duvall came rushing through the open door to throw her arms around a pleasantly surprised 'Investigator Montana', who hugged her right back.

'Oh, Duke, I had to see that you were all right.' She squeezed his arms and stepped back to look him up and down. 'You are all right, aren't you? You're not lying about that? You always did lie to me, you know.'

That was a dig about Sun River, but he didn't rise to the bait. He was more touched than he cared show to realize she still cared, even though it was all over between them.

'You know me, Bella, bulletproof but never proof against Cupid's arrow.'

'Well, who is your friend, Duke?'

'Enemy,' he corrected. 'Someone you don't want to know, honey.' He was reaching for his hat and steering her for the door. 'I'll walk you back. Er, you won't steal anything if I leave you here will you, Mr Polk? Remember the time in Pipeclay when you were arrested for lifting schoolchildren's play lunch . . . ? All those little kiddies with nothing to eat . . . scared by the bad man. Tsk, tsk.'

They were gone. Slowly the congested look left Polk's saturnine face. It galled him that Montana could get away with playing the fool and playing fast and loose with discipline the way he consistently did. His long-standing dislike for the man had just been upped several notches. But as he moved out onto the balcony to watch the couple making down the Union Street hill as though neither had a care in the world, he sighed gustily and admitted something to himself he'd never admit in anyone's hearing.

Montana was the man for the job. The only man.

And that being the case, it would be a betrayal of his responsibilities if he was to do anything other than forget his complaint and go ahead and support his aggravating field man.

He sat down heavily. Close friends envied his high position with the secret government intelligence organization, known only as the Bureau. Times like this he wondered why.

The fossicker called Klondyke leaned against his mule and squinted down the canyon where the diggers were slaving away feverishly as they'd done the day before, and a year ago come next Thanksgiving.

The Thanksgiving strike had been pure luck, he

knew; a wizened old Swede had dropped his knife in a brook, was scrabbling for it when he turned over a flatbed rock and saw the yellow winking up at him.

At first he'd thought it might have been fool's gold until he began beating up on it with a stone. That was the real test. Fool's gold wasn't knit together properly and would splatter into brittle pieces. But real gold was almost as soft as butter and would flatten out.

But the Swede was an old-stager who had to be doubly sure before he went running off to stake his claim and buy himself a pair of new britches. Firstly he got two bowls of water and a set of gimcrack scales. Using an equal amount of silver, he weighed both metals under water, the silver and his sample. The gold proved heavier. He tested his find with acid to see if it would corrode. It wouldn't. So began the Viking Mine which opened up the Dogwood Hills and old loner Klondyke hadn't known a peaceful day since.

Or a lucrative one, for that matter.

But today was a different kind of day insofar as he'd stumbled upon something that might prove to be the real thing. And not being a canny old Swede who'd spent his entire life panning one puddly creek or another until he'd finally got to be the richest man in the Territory, Klondyke, the suspicion-driven loner, needed to see some expert he could trust.

He showed up in Hellfire the following day when everybody was gossiping about some fellow getting shot to death. Klondyke wasn't interested in people much, just gold. Which was howcome he found himself standing a couple of doors along from a pint-sized office with the words SAFE CLAIMS painted on the window, where a baggy-panted digger just like himself was emerging with a pink claims form clasped in his grimy fist.

'Safe claims!' Klondyke snorted, was about to move off when the woman came to stand in the door-way, folded her arms under truly outstanding breasts and dropped him a cheeky wink.

'Help you, Cutie?'

Cutie? Klondyke had never been cute even as a newborn. He was gnarled, corroded, weather-stained, even smelt bad. But he had a chunk of pure yellow in his deep baggy pockets which he reckoned might transform him into the richest miner in the Dogwoods – providing he didn't let anyone cheat him out of it.

The Safe Claims lady, who looked suspiciously like a saloon queen to him, appeared too smart and friendly to be anything but shady to his rheumy eye. But God, she was beautiful. She was so damn pretty he started to ache all over and shake a little. So much so that she disappeared inside and came out a short time later with a glass of water, and introduced herself as Bella – which he was smart enough to known meant 'beautiful' in some furrin lingo.

She did her level best to talk him into filing claim on the creek which he hadn't even told her about. He now suspected she might be a saint, or at least an angel. But even when she took him inside and intro-duced him to her partner – a city slicker if he ever saw one – and fixed him coffee with a johnny cake –

he revealed nothing.

He hadn't come down in the last shower.

'That's OK, Klon,' she assured him, making for the door. 'You wouldn't believe just how many poor and raggedy old miners I get to lure into my little web just by standing out front looking innocent and breathing in deep – like this.'

It was a crime what that deep breath did to her – what could a decent man politely call it – upper body? It was all a bit much for an old and lonesome prospector who'd geared himself up at last to come get a licence for his claim, yet now found himself shying off, as he'd done before.

Suddenly weary, he dropped into a chair as hard-faced Ramont dealt with a customer – none too politely by the sound of him.

Trouble was, he really needed a licence.

Prospecting was permitted without a licence all over the country, but not digging and washing out. Klondyke had been working his secret claim, remote from the vast sprawl of the Dogwood Hills diggings and established mines, for several weeks. He thought he had something, knew he must be able to dig and wash, otherwise any sonuva could jump your claim and you didn't have a legal leg to stand on.

But there were problems with licences, big ones.

You had to go to an office licensed by the government and state exactly where your diggings were situated and pay a good sum – and he was broke. You also were required to surrender a portion of the yield, if any.

That wasn't the worst of it.

However careful you might be taking out a licence, you could almost guarantee the word would leak out somehow, and reach the ears of the bandits.

The trick of the skilled bandits was to lie in wait for their victims over weeks or even months while they did all the hard work, then drop on them like vultures out of a clear blue sky when they eventually set out for the bank with their poke.

What was a man to do?

'Hey!'

Klondyke glanced up. The woman's partner was glaring from behind a rickety desk. He had a pencil behind his ear and was shuffling licence forms.

'You buyin' or just lookin', bum?'

Klondyke was offended. 'I'm waitin' for the lady to come back.'

'Not in my office you ain't.' Ramont's nose twitched. Klondyke worked in water every day but was never tempted to bathe. 'C'mon, you're gone, goat-breath.'

So saying, Ramont came round the desk, seized him roughly by the collar and heaved him for the door. Klondyke tripped on the stoop and went down on his knees. Ramont rested a boot against his rump and shove-kicked him onto the walk just as a flashy-looking stranger happened by, giving Bella the thumbs up as he indicated the sign.

Montana's smile disappeared as he stopped himself from stumbling over the old sourdough.

'What the—?' he said, and hooking hold of a handful of collar, reefed the man to his feet, dusted him off and put a flat stare on the big man in the doorway.

'I saw that,' he rapped. 'What the hell is wrong with you?'

'What business is that of yours, Montana?'

'All right, all right.' Bella's voice broke in at just the right moment. Taking the old miner's arm, and holding up a warning finger to Duke, she swung on her partner. 'That was nasty, Buck. If you think this is any way to run a business, you're wrong.'

'We ain't in the bum business, Bell.'

'Go back inside.'

'What?'

'You heard.'

For a moment it seemed Ramont might defy her. But as a watching Montana well knew, Bella Duvall could be intimidating when the mood took her.

As Ramont vanished with a curse, Bella – the very name gave Klondyke goosebumps – took him by the elbow and was guiding him to a bench, her fragrance engulfing his bent and stringy-muscled old body like warm sunshine, and asking if he was all right.

'Looks all right to me, Bell,' remarked Montana. 'These old birds can be tough as rawhide, don't you know. Have a cigar, gramps. Steady you down.'

Klondyke blinked, staring upwards.

It was like he was dreaming. Here he was, a hard luck prospector, too suspicious to have a friend, too smelly to have a woman and too scared to buy a licence when he thought he might be onto some yellow stuff – being fussed over by a couple who looked like they'd stepped out of the pages of some fancy Eastern magazine, like *Harper's*, fussing over him as though he was someone important.

He made to reply but Duke shoved a stogie into his mouth and made a light with his pocket flint.

'So, how's business, Bella?' he enquired. It was the first time he'd stopped by. She was pleased but took pains to appear casual.

'Just fine. You?'

'Doing great.' Then Montana winked and smiled. 'You know, you're looking great.' He studied the prospector's road-map features. 'New boyfriend? Better than the one you arrived with.'

Tetchy Klondyke caught the irony.

'I ain't nobody's boyfriend,' he growled. He might be old and insanitary, but he was tough. 'Where'd you git that frilly shirt? Maisy's Millinery?'

Bella liked that. So did Montana. 'Nice to meet you old-timer . . . I think.' He slipped both hands in his pockets and turned to study the legend painted on the window. 'Safe Claims eh . . . ?'

'Now don't start,' Bella said with a warning look at the miner. 'Klondyke hasn't done any business with us, but he will in time. Isn't that so, Klonny?'

Now both were smiling at him, the dude a little mockingly, maybe, but smiling none the less. In that moment they presented the most dazzling picture of youth and beauty he'd ever seen, and the feeling that came over him was akin to that time in California at the diggings when, for a brief space of time, he'd thought a big gold rock he'd kicked over was the genuine article, not the fool's gold it eventually turned out to be.

It was as though after weeks and months in the rocky hills he was savoring life again.

He shoved a hand into his deep pocket. Felt it. Caressed it. Met Bella's smiling eyes. Was tempted, just for a moment, to say yes. Yes, he needed to buy a licence and stake an official claim; yes, he would trust an assayer if she recommended him; yes . . .

Then reality returned and his moment of weakness was gone. With a nod to the woman and a half-grin at Montana, he hitched his possibles sack over his shoulder and clomped away.

'Have you no shame, woman?' Duke smiled. 'Poor old geezer. How much would you expect to milk him for?'

'You're such a cynic.' Bella glanced up at him and, sure enough, his old familiar feeling immediately reared its ugly head again. He must ignore it. Polk was still around. The Bureau was growing impatient. He'd been through Hellfire with a fine-toothed comb, was figuring where to start searching next. This was no time for old feelings, or even a cup of make-up coffee. So, instead he took Bella by the arm and was steering her back for the office when Ramont came lunging out, white-faced and tight-lipped.

'Just what in hell do you think you're doing, goddamnit?' he barked. He grabbed for Bella's shoulder. 'Damnit, woman, you get back inside . . .'

His fingers closed on her shoulder and the edge of Montana's right hand chopped down on his wrist like a slamming door.

Everything happened at once.

Bella cried out, Ramont swore viciously and swung a whistling haymaker. Montana ducked under it and came up with his favorite punch, a short, jolting right hook that packed dynamite and connected flush with Ramont's jaw.

Bella's partner in commerce and stage staggered back through the office doorway, fell on his back with a crash and didn't move.

'Why you . . . !' she shrieked at Montana, and swung a blistering left hook of her own. He weaved low, caught her pretty fist in his hand like catching a baseball, whipped his free arm around her waist and kissed her fully on the mouth. Instinctively he turned his hip to catch the whipping knee intended for his groin.

'Easy, Bell, you'll chase the suckers away,' he panted. 'Your boy's not hurt . . . just resting . . .'

Klondyke had halted three doors down when he heard the ruckus erupt.

He peered intently to watch emotions chase one another across the woman's lovely face in rapid succession as the dude continued to hold her arm. Then to his astonishment he watched her eventually shrug, reach out and close the door on the unconscious Ramont, then calmly stroll off in the opposite direction with Montana, arm in arm, with the whole street gawking.

They seemed to him as wild and unpredictable as a pair of wild horses, free and not giving a damn.

Suddenly he felt great, envying nobody as he threw out his chest and headed off. That pair might have looks and high spirits and shine like the sun, but they didn't look rich, he consoled himself. Of course, he wasn't rich either. Not yet. But he was ready to stand up before all the glory-robed Judges of Heaven itself and swear on his immortal soul that he truly believed he had the best prospects in his long and ragged-assed life, right at this very moment. And hitched at his raggedy britches which were dragging down heavily on one side.

He was clutching at straws.

Duke Montana knew it the morning he rented a stiff-gaited claybank and set off across the railroad tracks to take the winding trail leading to one-horse Wolf River some ten miles out as the crow flies.

After having questioned every citizen and transient in town along with scores more from the spreads, farms and timber-leases within miles, all he'd encountered was the identical result. Shaking heads. He was beginning to smell a serious flaw in the Bureau's information that the missing North woman was anywhere in this region. But they'd given him Hellfire and he would exhaust it totally before admitting he was licked.

He forded a murmuring stream lined with watercress and picked up the trail again.

It was cold, with patches of snow in the woods, but he was dressed for it. No bench-made boots or silk cravats today, but rather moleskins, leather jacket and corduroy shirt. If unsuccessful at Wolf he planned to continue northward, likely ride as far as the Dogwoods and the mines and diggings.

He couldn't imagine any woman in her right mind

hiding out in a mining camp. But if Hannah North were still alive, then her past history suggested she might just be clever and desperate enough to come up with the totally unexpected.

He rode round a mighty oak which might have stood there when Lief Erickson berthed his dragon ship on New World soil, and took the trail for the Dogwood Hills.

CHAPTER 6

TROUBLE AT THE WHISKEY SHACK

'Purty woman that.'

'She is indeed. But have you seen her? Might go by the name of North.'

'Sorry, friend.'

'How about you, buddy?'

The second miner squinted at the photo in the wallet, shook his shaggy head. 'Nope. Say, you the feller they say's been lookin' all over for this here woman?'

Montana sighed.

He was standing on a slab of rock in the rough center of what had resembled, from a distance riding in, a vast disturbed ants' nest with busy shapes bustling to and fro all over the torn and turbulent landscape under a leaden sky in a chilly mountain air polluted by sweat, noise, cursing, braying, grinding, drilling and the sort of cussing that might well cause real ants to curl up and die.

The Dogwood Hills mining camp flowed for miles before him in all directions. There were several large tunnel mines with sprawling work-buildings, bunkhouses, processing-plants, engine sheds within short distance of the new railroad depot. Shaft mines proliferated, gouging deeper and deeper by the week. But by far the most prolific breed of human ant were the prospectors, the old-timers and the new hopefuls in their mud-spattered rig, all marked by the same look – the wide-eyed and slightly feverish stare of men staking everything on one blow of the pick, one glimmer in a stream, a breath of golden hope.

They looked insane to Duke, standing out amongst them in his quality riding-gear and handsome guns. But he felt anything but superior, for a change. For he shared the passion, understood the seductive lure, loved the notion of making the big strike and living like a goddamn Eastern potentate just as passionately as did any sweating, foot-freezing fanatic in any one of a dozen muddy streams and creeks.

The only difference between himself and the diggers was that, despite his love of wealth and gold, the dirt, disappointment and monotony of their life would surely kill him long before he had half a chance to make his strike.

He sighed and stepped over a sodden roadway to present his picture-wallet to the next bearded and hope-driven fool:

'Ever seen this woman . . . ?'

Hours later he was still at it.

In quantities that are worth going after, gold occurs in two ways: in veins in hard rock and in loose form in the soil. The veins occur in old fissures and bedrock, thrust up from the earth's interior. Over millions of years erosion wears away the rocks and exposes the mineral veins. Maybe a thousand men were scattered over some twenty or thirty low hills here, and with the day approaching dark down, a no-longer immaculate Montana reckoned he'd covered every one.

To no avail.

According to both boss Cullenmore and pompous Polk, Bureau intelligence remained convinced that missing Hannah North was still in Hellfire or the region. Intelligence had a habit of being right nine times out of ten.

They were also notoriously tight-lipped, he reflected, tight-lipped. A field man, on a job like this, was invariably furnished only with the bare essentials of information necessary for him to be able to pursue a case effectively with a reasonable hope of success.

No more than that.

You could be driven crazy by not knowing all you reckoned you should, but rarely would they relent and open up.

This secrecy could drive an investigator loco even though he might well accept the reason behind it. The theory was, that if you were captured by the enemy and put to the torture, you couldn't reveal what you didn't know. And on some jobs, like this one, you were warned that your assignment involved national security.

About all he'd been able to glean about the bigger picture was that it was something to do with the upcoming elections which would see a new adminis- tration installed in Capital City, which by itself was roughly no help at all.

The Dogwoods had been about his last hope. Now he was heading back to report to stiff-necked Polk that this was one of Intelligence's one-out-of-ten failures.

On his way back to the sprawl of the Viking Mine, where he'd left his horse, he sighted a miner he mistook for Klondyke. This prompted him to ask after the man; maybe he might know something.

The mud-caked humanoid he questioned just grinned and shook his head.

'You won't find old Klondyke, mister. Comes and goes like a ghost, so he does.' His gesture encom- passed the denuded hills, the woods and faraway mountains. 'We all reckon he's got somethin' out there, but if he has he sure ain't lettin' nobody in on it. Not that I blame him of course,' he added with a concerned look. 'The gold bandits are about these days. Old Syd yonder reckons he spied a bunch up on the ridge there a day or two back . . . evil mongrel sons of bitches. . . .'

He didn't bother asking anyone else; not about Hannah North or the old prospector. This was one burnt-out field man who made his way back at last to the Viking, where he made himself known to the mine boss who agreed to put him up for the night, for a price, but then relented and invited him to supper.

There were a few places down along the OK Trail that he might check on his way back tomorrow, he told himself as he availed himself of a spare room and bed in the mine boss's comfortable quarters. After that he would be able to face Polk and tell him flat that their young woman had to be someplace else in Cascade County – if she was still alive. He was beginning to doubt it.

The early winter morning had a bite in it. Powdery snow sifted across the rugged landscape, coming to rest finally in a windbreak in the trees. On the lee side of the pines, six gray-brown birds huddled in a grassy furrow, waiting for the climbing sun to generate some heat.

A hoof clipped stone.

In an instant the birds burst into the air to go beating down along a long avenue in the spruces, russet cheeks and gray breasts accenting the horseshoe-shaped band of chestnut feathers that identified each one.

He hadn't smiled much so far today but did so as he watched the covey of Hungarian partridges clear the timber and soar up into the sun, reminding him there was more to life than hard work, high risk and slow investigations.

He'd seen plenty that was interesting but nothing that seemed valuable at the diggings. The reason he was taking the OK Trail back down to the valley lands was because he'd not covered it before, not that he expected much of it now.

He doubted that anyone, much less a young

93

woman alone, would seek refuge up here on this wind-haunted flank of the hills where mighty trees were blowing about in the thin sunlight with a constant eerie whispering that would spook a dog wolf.

Some five miles downtrail he glimpsed a rooftop through the trees. The Jacks had told him about the Whiskey Shack trailhouse. Good place to find a feed, a drink or a fight, or so they claimed.

He was thinking about Polk as he guided the horse up to the hitch rail. He didn't know if his contact man would still be in town when he got back. Polk never revealed anything he wasn't compelled to. He did know the man would have been in touch with the Bureau by wire. He supposed he was lucky Cullenmore regarded him highly, reckoned that if that weren't the case Polk would have engineered his dismissal long since, despite his record. Polk considered him a dilettante, a flashgun-artist attracted only by the excitement and money of the field man's life, with none of his so-called sense of duty. In turn, Duke saw the lofty Englishman as someone obsessed by power, authority, protocol and procedure rather than results.

But there was a plus to their flinty relationship. Perversely, Montana found Polk's antagonism a spur for him to succeed. Which he did, more often than he failed. He still didn't intend to have this assignment end in failure even if it was proving one of his most difficult yet.

He stepped down and climbed the muddied steps. The doors had been tied back in mute welcome to

94

the thirsty traveller, and he saw figures in miner's blue rolling dice, a big man seated alone at a table in a gloomy corner, a bartender polishing glasses, and Silleck.

He recognized the slim-bodied man in the blood-red shirt from Hellfire. Had been unable to find out much about him, but knew he had him tagged right. Trouble. Well, as he and trouble were old partners that surely wouldn't deter him from seeking what he'd come here for, namely a stiff whiskey and information, in that order.

He sensed the Whiskey Shack quieten noticeably as he walked to the bar and spun a shiny double eagle on the scarred top.

'Carry Godfather's?' he asked.

'What's that?'

'Never mind. Two fingers of what you've got.'

His drink arrived and he flipped the little black wallet from his pocket, fingered it open.

'Ever seen her, barkeep?'

The man looked, shook his head. 'Sorry, mister. Quite a looker, ain't she?'

'She is that,' he said, pocketing his change. And added under his breath, *Or was* . . .

At least he knew they were trying to kill her whoever 'they' might be. He was sure the Bureau could provide more information on who was pulling the strings that might get to strangle Hannah North. But as usual they only ever gave you as much as they thought you needed to know to get the job done and no more. Field men were entrusted with big respon-sibilities but were rarely completely trusted.

95

Particularly ones whom personnel bosses might regard as show ponies.

He picked up his drink and was turning away from the bar when someone spoke.

'Mind if I take a look?'

He knew it was Silleck who'd spoken before he turned, even though he'd never heard the man's voice before. The voice fitted the body it came from; sleek, silky, challenging.

Wordlessly he produced the picture. Silleck took the wallet, held the picture up to the window-light, stared at it, stared back at him.

'Nope. Mind me askin' who she might be?'

'Just a missing woman,' Duke said, replacing the wallet in his breast pocket. He wanted to end the conversation at that point but Silleck lingered, studying him with a mixture of intensity and lurking amusement, which irritated. But he refused to let his annoyance show. He was working. He was at the office. But he was getting desperate for leads, any leads from anyplace.

'Sure her face doesn't ring a bell?' he pressed.

The man leaned his supple back against the bar edge and hooked a boot over the rail.

'Said it didn't, didn't I?'

Someone cleared his throat loudly and Montana turned to see the large man in the corner rising from his table to come forwards.

'What's wrong?' Silleck challenged the other. 'We're just talkin'.'

It was as if he'd not spoken. The big man with the Slavic features, a wisp of mustache and tiny ice-blue eyes, rested a hand on the bar and studied Montana thoughtfully. Now he was sure the customers had gone silent. He gave the man stare for stare but didn't speak. Always make them speak first. Gave you an advantage.

'Mr Montana,' he said at length, 'I've heard about you and your search for this—'

That was as far as he got when a rear door banged open and a heavyset man who seemed vaguely familiar emerged from a back room, lurching a little, plainly riled about something and obviously soused, even at this early hour.

'So, this is the mucker, is it?' he slurred, approaching with swinging arms. 'The dude what reckons he's something special. So, where's your top hat and cane today, Montana?'

'Shut your mouth!' said the big man, not raising his voice. 'Keep it shut.'

The voice carried authority but it seemed the newcomer was too far gone to heed. He was enraged about something, seemed bent on venting it. Montana set his glass aside as he lumbered at him, let him swing one that missed by a mile. Then he deliberately lined him up with a light left tap to the nose and followed up with a pile-driving right to the point that sounded whip-crack loud. The drunk went down like something made of blubber.

Silence.

The Whiskey Shack didn't even seem to breathe as Montana backed up and dropped a hand to gun handle. He was pretty certain by now he wasn't going to gather any information here, might even land himself in deeper trouble if he stayed on. He didn't see what was to be gained. And he was determining whether he went or stayed. His hand on his Colt and his finger on the trigger proclaimed it.

Silleck and the big man both looked proddy now, but they also knew who was holding top cards. For now.

Yet Silleck's affronted pride and vanity made him reckless in the face of personal danger.

'Want me to deal with the bastard?' he demanded aggressively.

'Maybe another time.' The big man jerked his head at Montana, indicated the tied-back doors. 'Riding time.'

He backed slowly for the doors. He felt fine. Nothing like whacking someone to get you relaxed. As he reached the doors, Silleck and the big man began arguing heatedly. He picked up some words but couldn't figure exactly what was being said. Nobody tried to impede him as he moved to the horse, untied it, stepped up and rode off for the trail.

It was as he was moving out of earshot that something he'd half-heard Silleck say in his anger registered belatedly. He'd called the *hombre* he was arguing with, 'Dimitri'.

Riding fast and deep in thought, Montana didn't hear the cry from the woods at first. Linking Silleck and the man the hardcase had called 'Dimitri' convinced him beyond any doubt that he'd just made contact with the rest of the gang he'd traded lead with down at Prairie Valley the day before boarding the stage up to Hellfire. And with that certainty he focused his suspicions on the man he'd just knocked on his ass, straining his recollection of what he'd seen during the shootout at the Territory Hotel. Could that drunk have been the second man on the roof outside his window that night?

'Hey! Hey, mister!'

That shout eventually penetrated his thoughts. Reining in abruptly, he turned and glimpsed a figure standing by a horse some thirty yards distant in the timber. He was waving, and there seemed to be something or someone half-visible against a big old deadfall in back of him.

'What?' he yelled impatiently. He was fired up to get back to town in record time. He wanted to get to the library, speak to the sheriff about Silleck and a man called Dimitri, confront Polk, get a wire off to the Bureau. 'I'm in a hurry, damnit! What's going on?'

'Found a man hurt here, mister. Looks like a miner.'

Duke cursed, kicked the horse and rode in through the sad trees to rein in by the deadfall. The man was standing before what looked at first like a pile of crumpled dirty clothing. Then the pile stirred and became a man lifting his pain-racked face to stare up at him, and Montana heard himself hiss: 'Klondyke. What the tarnation . . . ?'

Klondyke it was, a Klondyke who looked like he'd tumbled into a millrace up at the diggings, judging by the blood and bruises. His clothes were half-ripped off his pale old body and he spat a mouthful of blood when he tried to speak.

'Heard all this moanin' as I was ridin' by,' supplied the man who'd attracted his attention. His horse was festooned with sturdy leather bags and he wore the shoulder badge of the US Mail. 'He seems to know you, mister.'

Still resentful over the delay but managing at least to half-hide it, Duke jumped down and, with the help of the mailrider, managed to get the complaining old man up onto the deadfall, where he checked him out for injuries while he began to wheeze out a few words.

'Camp bandits . . .' he croaked. 'Jumped me on my way to my claim . . . tried to beat it out of me where it was . . .' He broke off with a gasp of pain as Duke used his belt to strap his injured arm to his body. He seemed to muster a grimacing smile of pride as he went on. 'Told 'em nothin, not even my name.' He indicated his scattered belongings in the nearby brush. 'They went through everythin' just as if they believed I'd made a strike. Well, they beat me up good, and I must've passed out and—'

'Yeah, OK, we'll hear the rest when we get you to the doc's,' Montana broke in. 'Mailman, can you . . . ?'

'Hell no,' the man protested. 'I'm an hour behind schedule already. I got to be on my rounds . . . so if you wouldn't mind, Mr Montana . . . ?'

Montana was right when he disclaimed any links with Samaritanism. Times like this he could be tough and selfish and put duty ahead of everything else. But he had to concede he wouldn't even leave a dog behind, beat up like the old geezer was.

100

So he loaded him up on his mule and set off for the town, yet barely stopped cursing under his breath during the full two hours it took to cover the distance to the St Leque Street surgery, by which time his patient was just about out to it from the pain, but still talkative.

'You're a real brick, son,' he panted as the medico and his nurse assisted him inside. 'When I first seen you I reckoned – now there's a flash artist if ever I seen one—'

'Sure, sure.' Montana was already on his way out. 'Whatever you say. Much obliged, doc, *adios.*'

'I won't forget this,' Klondyke promised, then broke off with a sputter and a foul curse. The nurse, who looked a tough one, was already starting to scrub him down with a flannel of lye soap. He hated being clean with a passion, but it was when the no-nonsense woman attempted to remove his big thick-soled boots that he went really loco, so much so that in the end they had to allow him to keep them on while the doctor went over him to see what was broken.

They thought he was loco, and maybe he was.

By the time Polk had decoded his latest telegraph message received from the Bureau it was time for him to have his mustache trimmed. He could do it himself but preferred to have someone else handle the chore. In truth, wherever lackeys or menials could be utilized, the Bureau's personnel boss not only preferred their services but actively sought them out. He liked having people run after him, it made him feel important and respected – the kind of response

101

he didn't necessarily receive from all field men.

He scowled at that thought and rang the bell that summoned the barber to his room at the hotel. While the man was busy with his clippers Polk managed to scan the message again, his frown cutting deeper.

Cullenmore was unhappy at what he termed his 'apparently total lack of progress', and forcefully reminded Polk that this was the reason he'd been dispatched to Hellfire in the first place. Not a word of censure of investigator Montana, of course. It was all Polk's fault. In closing, the head man even had the gall to recommend Polk 'get cracking and stop procrastinating' on the North case.

His toilet completed, he donned sober dark coat and bowler hat and set off purposefully for the Territory Hotel at the head of Union Street. Doubtless Montana had returned late from the Dogwood Hills, had probably decided to 'unwind' at the Silver Palace and, if history was anything to go on, hadn't retired until around dawn.

Well, like it or not, that was one field man who was going to furnish him a full and complete report by nine, or Polk would want to know the reason why.

Nothing about Hellfire pleased Polk. The boom town in the valley was too coarse, crude and rough around the edges for his tastes. He was accustomed to much better. Although the premises which housed the Bureau on a deliberately ordinary Capital City backstreet appeared drab and even neglected from the outside, the interior was plush and even luxurious, his own suite of rooms in particular were lavishly furnished and meticulously operated. He had a house in the hills where he dined off fine Irish linen and boasted both a maid for his wife and a gentleman's helper for himself.

Back there, Polk lived almost like the upper-class English gentleman he was. It seemed a long way from Hellfire, Cascade County.

Here on operations a man encountered all sorts of primitive conditions, inferior food, lousy service and boorish individuals such as Sheriff Dunstan, as well as the buck-toothed telegrapher, and the dullard who clipped his steel-grey mustache every morning at exactly eight-thirty.

All Montana's fault, of course. It was his firm belief that, had his personal *bête noir* among field men not spent so much time gambling, showing off, wenching and whatever, the North case might well be closed by this and they could both be gone from here, hopefully in opposite directions.

His breath was laboring by the time he'd climbed the hill to reach the Territory. Too many cigars and nervous tension. He scowled as he paused to catch his breath and peer up at the sloping roof where an ugly russet-colored stain remained as a reminder of a recent deadly event. He might have liked to hold Montana responsible for that incident, but in all conscience knew he couldn't.

He was brusque with the maid when he instructed her to conduct him to guest Montana's suite. The woman seemed confused and reluctant to follow orders. She fussed and carried on but Polk would brook no delay.

'Mr Montana's room!' he repeated, brandishing

103

his furled brolly, and Cissy caved in and conducted him meekly upstairs. She tapped on the door of Room 22, called Montana's name as she eased it open in response to his muffled reply, then shot off downstairs like a cat taking the short cut through the dogyard.

With squared shoulders and clenched jaw Polk strode through the door to reach the center of the spacious lounge which gave onto the bedroom whose big glass doors stood wide open. Then he stopped on a dime.

'What the devil . . . ?'

His first thought was that the stupid woman had shown him into the wrong suite. He was quickly disabused of that notion when the man in the satin robe seated on the huge double bed with his back to him, turned his head and he saw it was indeed his field man.

He blinked.

The stunning blonde woman in the revealing negligée, propped up against several huge pillows to complete this scene of tranquil domesticity, was the same blonde who'd apparently pulled a gun on Montana in the stagecoach that had carried both to town: Bella Duvall.

'Well, don't just stand there, man,' Montana said nonchalantly. 'Coffee's on the side table. Help yourself. Bella and I have something to finish.'

The blood drained from Polk's prominent features. Something to finish? Surely even Montana didn't intend . . . ? He sighed in relief when his man rose and passed the woman her robe. Suddenly the

104

visitor needed coffee. Black. Lots of it.

'Respectable, darling?' asked Montana.

'Regrettably, yes . . . darling.'

They strolled into the lounge arm in arm as Polk's color slowly returned. From shocked gray his complexion turned bright pink. That robe wouldn't cover a . . . well, it certainly didn't cover all of Miss Duvall, that was dead certain.

'To what do we owe the pleasure?' Montana said off-handedly, taking cigarettes from his pocket.

'I, ah, didn't mean to intrude, investigator Montana. Perhaps we could conduct this meeting elsewhere?'

'No, let's get it over with. Bella honey, would you pour me some coffee?'

'Whatever you say – honey.'

It went downhill from there. Polk managed to convey the thrust of the Bureau's latest directive, while Montana in turn reported on his less than successful visit to the workings, capped off by his clash with two men 'of interest', namely Silleck and Dimitri, whom he now connected directly with the first phase of his investigation – the pursuit of, and eventual clash with the gang believed to have been searching for Hannah North in the region prior to his arrival.

Montana then went on to hint at a possible vital lead he meant to follow up first thing this morning. Oddly, Polk showed little interest as he took up hat and brolly, invited his man to contact him at the jail-house later, and excused himself. This was all a bit much for him. As far as he'd understood it, Montana and 'Miss Duvall' had been at daggers drawn ever since their conspicuous arrival in town together. As a consequence, this scene of tranquil domesticity and implied lust was more than he could endure at this time of day, and then some.

The door closed behind his rigid back. Bella giggled and linked her arms round Duke's neck as he collected his shaving-gear.

'I'm afraid we shocked your boss, Duke.'

'He's easily shocked. But he's not my boss.'

'Not your boss . . . of what?' she probed.

He disengaged himself with a smile. 'You know I can't tell you that, Bell.'

'Always so secret and mysterious. All right, I won't press you. I just though that, after last night . . .'

'Last night was due to happen since the moment I clapped eyes on you. You know that as well as I do. And with luck we can keep it this way. And that means no questions . . . sugar plum.'

'OK,' she agreed, pouring coffee from a big brass pot. 'But just remember, whenever all this hush-hush stuff raises its head, I automatically think of Sun City where I never really knew what was going on until suddenly one day you just disappeared and left me high and dry. Is that likely to happen again?'

He took her in his arms, dead serious now.

'Honey, all I can tell you about Sun City is that I was in deep trouble there. People were out to nail me, and if they'd caught me with you they'd have killed us both. Will you accept that?'

'Of course,' she purred silkily, licking his chin like a cat. 'But what you must accept, Duke Montana, is that if you deliberately go out of your way to hurt or

106

deceive me again, I'll finish what I started on the stage. With the same gun. Do you believe what Bella says, snookums?'

He looked into her eyes. They glittered like jewels. But in their depths he saw she meant every word.

'What's the situation with lover boy?' he asked, changing the subject.

'Well, until you came calling last night it was cooling but still working.' She smiled carelessly, shrugged unconcernedly. 'He bores me now. I'll let him take over the office and I'll concentrate on the shows.'

'He strikes me as a joker who could turn pretty mean if he tried.'

'He's a bum.' She reached up and linked her hands behind his neck. 'I realized I was tired of him when you knocked him flat and I thought – good! Are you sure you have to rush off . . . ?'

He kissed her lightly. He didn't know if it would last five minutes or five months. Their relationship, even in Sun City, had never been like most people's. They made no promises, saw other people, played by the free and easy rules of the fast-moving and hard-playing new society of the West. But Montana suspected that if he were ever to fall in love – and that was a big if – it would likely be with someone like the unpredictable and exciting Bella Duvall.

But right now he had another female on his mind.

'Deal,' he said. 'Now I have to shave. I've an appointment at nine.'

'Where?'

'At the library.'

'Now that's a lie if ever I heard one.'

'No, Gospel truth,' he insisted. And it was.

The librarian was young and skinny in a bright-blue dress with big yellow dandelions all over it.

'I'm sorry, Mr Montana, but Mrs Jones resigned three days ago. Is it about books? May I assist you?'

'But . . . but she can't be gone,' he protested, looking around. 'She's been here two years . . .' He broke off, realizing the girl would have no reason to lie. 'Where can I find her? I'm a friend, and this is urgent.'

He was given an address on a back street not far from the railroad depot. He left in a hurry, uneasy without even knowing why.

The notion he was following up had come to him up at the diggings the night he'd sat going through his journal by lanternlight, looking over his daily records, searching for something, anything, no matter how small, that he might have overlooked.

He'd turned out the lantern convinced that, in retrospect, the incident that had seen staid Mrs Jones trailing him late at night on the street to beg him emotionally to quit his search for Hannah North had been strange and very much out of character. He'd come back to town determined to find out why this had seemed so important to her, what her interest in the missing woman could be.

He found the run-down house where Norah Jones had lived deserted. A neighbor informed him that the woman had simply come home one evening, packed and left by cab. She had left no forwarding address.

By the time he'd finished scouring the two-room

shack without finding much that could be construed as a lead, he was convinced his belated hunch was right. This was abnormal behaviour. What interest could a simple librarian have in the party he was hunting? And why would she suddenly quit and simply disappear?

He was about to quit the building when something on the floor he'd stepped over several times caught his eye. He'd mistaken it for a gray swab cloth in the poor light, only now realized it was something else, half-obscured by paper. He picked it up, turned it over, blinked.

It was a woman's long wig he was holding. A gray wig.

Gray?

Who would want a gray wig? Mrs Jones was already gray as goose-feathers. What use could she have had for a thing like this? Why would anyone want a gray wig . . . unless it was to look older . . . or maybe just different. . . .

Slowly he sat down on a worn chair with a cracked seat and conjured up a mental picture of the librarian. Frumpy, lumpy, ill-fitting dresses, not a skerrick of powder or paint, big black hornrims – gray and untidy hair.

Then, concentrating hard, he jumped up and began pacing. He forced himself to recall her voice, which upon reflection hadn't seemed all that old, he realized now. Then there was the way she'd moved the night she came after him, almost quick and even graceful in contrast with her customary plodding manner.

And he kept coming back to the puzzle. Who – particularly a woman – would go out of her way to look older and plainer than she really was?

He halted abruptly, eyes widening as the answer hit.

Who else but a woman who didn't want to be recognized?

CHAPTER 7

THE HUNTERS RIDE

'Montana!'

August made the name sound like a curse. He spat it at them accusingly as though holding them directly responsible for their situation, and maybe they were, to a degree. But Silleck, the volatile one with the touchy pride, wouldn't take too much from anyone, not even the man who paid their wages and had in fact recruited all present, along with the two who had died over the past ten days. Montana again.

'You didn't give us the go-ahead to finish off the son of a bitch if we was to bump into him accidental,' Silleck retorted, pacing up and down the way he did when agitated. 'Likely, if we'd made a serious try for him at the Trailhouse, you'd be griping on account of we were drawing too much attention to ourselves. Better get it clear in your head what you want – big man.'

Nobody spoke.

Iron-jawed August was a man of natural authority. Until this moment he'd had no real difficulty with his hired hands. Dimitri was a dangerous man, as were they all, but was mostly placid and respectful. Brodie, brother of the man Montana had blasted off the rooftop of the Territory Hotel, was all bluster and bad temper. The man showed eager to get after Montana and get square for what had happened up in the hills, but wasn't a man likely to cause trouble.

Only Silleck would, and was.

'OK, OK.' August was riled but wouldn't let it show. Too much was at stake. Of a sudden he'd been made to realize the operation was in danger of coming apart at the seams. Sounding off or even firing people now was no longer an option.

Election day was just around the corner; Singleman's whistle-stop campaign due to show up in Hellfire any any time; the North woman still missing. And now Montana was acting more and more like the man who spearheaded the enemy, who had to be taken out if they were to achieve their goal, namely find that bitch and shut her mouth for ever.

'Where is he now?' he rapped. They were gathered in a back room of the Indian Queen which commanded a view of the horse yards in back and the citizens going about their business along Wagon Street beyond.

'Seen him hustling towards Poor Town on my way here to meet you, boss,' supplied Dimitri.

'Anyone with him?'

'No, just him and his big swole-headed notion of

112

himself by the looks.'

As August paused to massage his chin, Silleck weighed in:

'Seems to me we've been doin' this thing kid-gloved. Soon as we figured he was the bastard who'd dogged us to Prairie Valley and shot Wade, we should've gone after him and cancelled his ticket.'

'Maybe so.' August's mind was racing. The job he'd been given was to find Hannah North and kill her. But it was to be done without fuss, preferably without anyone knowing, for there was a huge degree of political sensitivity concerning the whole matter. Thus far he'd followed orders, kept his men in check, had worked them hard at the search, but without success. He'd known early that Montana was also on the woman's trail but had been confident they would find her first, do what had to be done, then either bury Montana with her or simply forget about him, depending on whether his employers still considered the man a danger.

But Silleck was right, surely. They'd underestimated that high-roller, had paid the price, and now were running out of time.

'Find him,' August stated flatly. 'Flush him, report back and we'll hit him just as quick and quiet as we can – all of us.'

Silleck's grin was genial as he made for the door.

'Now you're talkin', boss man. Only thing, you should've told us this days ago—'

'Don't push your luck,' August snapped.

'Who needs luck?' Silleck asked rhetorically, going out. 'I had that slicker's number from the jump.' He

LAST STAGE TO HELLFIRE

paused and jabbed a finger east where a column of dirty gray smoke was puffing above the rooftops. 'Hey, looks like the governor's train is dead on time.'

'Governor to be,' August corrected. 'He's not elected yet and mightn't ever be if we don't do our job right.'

They glanced back at him uncomprehendingly before moving off in different directions. The hard-cases knew there was some connection between what they were doing and Singleman's campaign, but had no idea what it might be. They could only speculate it had to be linked with Miss Hannah North, some-how.

'And so, dear friends,' boomed the speaker from the rear observation platform of his gaily decorated Pullman car, 'when you vote for me you are voting for everything our wonderful Territory has always craved yet never really had. Namely straight-talking and honest government, progress, prosperity for everybody and – most important of all – an end to corruption in high places!'

They cheered him to the echo as he rammed his fists above his head, a portly, sweating man with silver hair of senatorial length, with that rare talent of telling you something and making you really believe it.

For too long it had seemed that the state house in Capital City had been buffeted by allegations of corruption in high places, power politics, shady deals and even – God forbid – a low simmering shadow over this eloquent, impressive man standing before them today; rumors linking him with, of all things, the illicit supply of arms to Indians.

But just looking and listening here by the railroad tracks, any citizen would realize that that just had to be evil rumor put abroad by Singleman's political enemies.

'Let's hear it for the Judge!' bawled the town sheriff, and the candidate mopped his brow with a white silk kerchief and drew in a big breath before launching into a full-blooded attack on the incumbent governor whom he'd vowed to unseat, not for his own aggrandisement but for the good of this wonderful Territory and his loyal, true friends, the people.

The lean rider astride the hard-breathing claybank came out of the brush with a grunt of relief, drew rein just short of the slope's sudden rimline.

Montana immediately leapt to ground and commenced quartering the area afoot. The tracks of the single horse with the diamond-head nails in its shoes, which he'd followed some five miles northwest of the town, had vanished in the brush. He needed to pick them up again even though the lie of the land suggested she would have cut south-west from here.

The librarian. Mrs Jones. Seemed she did a lot of riding on her Sundays away from the library, or at least so the liveryman had informed him. Eventually.

He paused by a jackpine thicket and absently sucked his knuckles. There were times in this business when he hated what he did, or had to do. The liveryman, for instance. In his little one-man stables-

LAST STAGE TO HELLFIRE

and-forge operation at the head of the street where Mrs Jones lived – or had done – the man had stubbornly insisted he'd had no recent dealings with the woman, hadn't rented her a horse that day, had no knowledge of her comings and goings. Knew nothing at all that could be of any use to Mr Montana, he was sorry to say.

But a neighbor of the librarian had informed Duke of her riding habits, and the livery was the obvious place for her to secure a horse. But even more tellingly, amongst the hoof – and man – tracks of the livery he'd already detected a woman's prints in the mud.

So he knocked the fellow down and asked him again.

He'd apologized afterwards, but only when the groggy liveryman admitted he'd 'forgotten' he'd rented Mrs Jones her regular roan saddle horse, the one shoed with diamond-head nails, and a soft mouth which suited a woman rider.

Another time, he would have tried added persuasion, or maybe a bribe to get what he wanted. But there was a strong sense of urgency now. He was concerned about his quarry and worried she could be actually fleeing the region, so had had to cut corners where he could.

He grunted in satisfaction when he eventually cut the tracks again. Heading south, like he'd figured.

He hit leather and dug. By force of long habit he kept glancing back as the claybank carried him smoothly along a gently winding course where the wind had piled beech leaves into golden drifts against hedges of bracken fern studded with rowan berries, red as blood in the autumn light.

The woods stretched as far as the eye could see and he rode through them swiftly until the sign veered away abruptly to his left and began to climb.

He reined in sharply a half-mile further on as the timber suddenly fell away to reveal the rising narrow trail curving round the base of a sloped cliff some thirty to forty feet high against which, some hundred yards ahead, stood a battered old woodman's cottage.

Nothing moved up there. He would have surveyed the scene longer but for his sense of urgency. It looked a likely hideout, lonesome, remote, some ten miles from town by his calculations.

No sign of life.

Until he heeled forward.

The crash of the rifle came shockingly loud. The puff of smoke billowing from a side window was still rising as he wheeled the horse back the way he'd come and vanished.

It was some thirty minutes later before Montana came easing along the narrow rock trail afoot on the opposite side of the cabin, shielded from its sight by the bulge of the cliff. His horse was well hidden below and he had a sixshooter in hand as he paused to squint round the shoulder at the building, trying to decide whether to call or risk moving in.

He decided on the latter course. It was late afternoon and already growing gloomy here in the lee of the cliff. There was but one window on his side of the cabin. He could keep a sharp eye on it and be ready

117

to hurl himself off the trail into the brush if she should suddenly appear with her rifle.

He knew it was her. The roan was partially visible in the stall. The shot had surprised, but the bullet hadn't come even remotely close, suggesting she had simply wanted to drive him off.

Way too late for that.

He waited a minute before darting forward. Cat-quick and silent, he made it to the side porch without incident, then ducked into the narrow space between the cliff and the cabin rear. Here he almost cannoned into the woman as she hurried out the rear door, toting a saddlebag over one arm and a rifle in the other.

It wasn't the librarian.

That was all he had time to register before throwing himself after her as she made to get back inside. She attempted to slam the door but he got his shoulder to it, drove it open then managed to get purchase on the back of her blouse as she tried to run. She whirled and struck at him furiously as his momentum drove her off-balance and they tumbled to the floor.

He landed atop her. She struck at him with clenched fists, connected. He didn't even notice, his jaw hanging open. From a distance of just a few inches he was staring into the unmistakable face of Hannah North.

It was good coffee he was drinking. This was an abandoned, secret place she'd discovered on her long Sunday rides a long time ago, she'd revealed, and she

118

had equipped it for all her needs. Out here for, sometimes, a full day at a time, she could be twenty-three years old Hannah North, daughter of the former and now deceased county attorney of Capital County, Ira J North.

She was calm now; she had surrendered. Yet it had taken Montana some considerable time after their one-sided wrestling match on the cabin floor to convince her – really convince her – that he was not one of the assassins who'd murdered her father and who had been hunting for her throughout the past two years, and never more threateningly than over the past couple of months.

He couldn't reveal exactly who he was but seemed to have convinced her he was connected to the law, that his purpose in hunting her as he'd done had been to simply find her and make her safe from those his superiors knew to be after her.

Naturally, he was intensely curious to hear her story, for he'd not heard it from the Bureau. They'd only told him as much as they considered he needed to know in order to locate her. He wanted to know the full story, both to round out his understanding of the case, as well as to get one back on Polk.

So he gave her time and turned on the charm until Mrs Jones, née Hannah North – this handsome slender young woman unrecognizable from her padded, dowdy, gray-wigged *alter ego* – was at last prepared to accept him at face value, and told him what he wanted to hear.

It had begun in the Mystic Mountains region almost three years before when Territory Rangers had intercepted an illicit shipment of rifles and carbines destined for a tribe of warring Cheyennes. County Attorney North had been drawn into the governmental investigation which had resulted, and after some time it had become increasingly plain that several wealthy and powerful men of affairs might have been involved, including power broker Nathan T. Singleman.

North's subsequent enquiries uncovered the fact that Singleman had extensive involvement in pressure groups, political kickbacks and carpetbagging on a large and probably unlawful scale. But North concentrated on the Cheyenne rifles and eventually came up with enough evidence and hearsay to convince him that a full scale formal investigation should be implemented.

He had not been surprised when Singleman had approached him and asked him to drop the case, protested his innocence, and offered him money.

It was the bribe offer that offended North, who promptly moved to get the investigation under way.

A week later his junior attorney was found shot dead in a Capital City back alley with a note saying BE WARNED pinned to his chest.

Fearful for his daughter's safety, North sought extended leave and vanished with Hannah, but continued with his investigative work, in which he was assisted by the Bureau. At the end of some five weeks, Hannah and her father were taking an evening stroll in a small town outside the capital when they were set upon by the gunmen who had killed the attorney. This time they shot her father dead and almost succeeded in killing her.

Amongst the killer gang she saw Singleman.

Traumatized and convinced that the law could not protect her, Hannah disappeared, living the life of a fugitive for several months before arriving in Hellfire complete with padded suits, hornrims and a dreary gray wig which gave her the appearance of a staid, dour woman of middle years who, so the library board said after she applied for her position there, seemed ideally suited.

She'd enjoyed eighteen months of a secret but incident-free existence until a month ago when a man named Silleck had shown up from somewhere asking after her. She had not slept since, and when Montana arrived out of noplace with his photograph, she realized that her time was up, that she must simply await the right moment, then vanish to start running again.

She concluded by saying that, although she felt she could believe him, she now felt beyond caring even if he should turn out to be one of 'them', the killers.

'And who do you think they might be, Hannah?' he asked.

'Singleman's thugs, of course. Who else? I have the documentary evidence gathered by my father in a strongbox at the Hellfire Bank that would destroy him, and he knows it. The fear of that evidence being presented must have been hanging over his head too long, and he's made a decision: that he must destroy it, and me, before he can ever get to enjoy his success.'

He nodded. It all added up. Singleman had the badmen, the money and the motivation to mount

121

such an action. But he would not succeed.

He rose and went to the windows to survey their surrounds. All was quiet as the early darkness came down. He turned and gave her a reassuring smile.

'I've got a horse down in the draw. We'll move out at dark and make for town to contact my boss. He'll second the assistance of the sheriff and we'll go after these men and take them down. Trust me. You'll be safe, Hannah.'

The words were barely out when a heavy caliber bullet smashed a window barely inches away, sending him lunging at the girl to hurl them both to the floor while the glass was still raining down.

CHAPTER 8

GUNFLAME

The bullet hammered into the doorjamb with the impact of a flung javelin, missing a crouching Montana by inches. It caromed away with a high-pitched whine before smacking into the cliff face and spraying rock fragments wide.

Hunkered low and breathing hard, he gazed upwards. A thin snow was beginning to fall out of the darkening sky and the cold bit deep. He turned to the cliff. All he was able to make out of the climbing figure was the faint light hue of her riding-britches, as tiny fragments of loosened stone came clattering down. But she hadn't fallen, as she'd feared, was steadily inching higher.

'Good girl!' he whispered. And wondered how many young women would undertake to climb a cliff face in near darkness with snow making surfaces slippery, and killers closing in below. Proved what North's daughter was made of, how she'd come to survive the past two years of what must have been hell.

'Throw down your guns and show yourself, dude!' a familiar voice hollered. 'We don't want you, only the bitch!'

Silleck sounded impatient.

They'd come in so quick that, but for the descending dark and having the cliff right there at the door in back, Montana and Hannah North would have been trapped like rats in the cabin. He supposed he was part-way trapped out here by the horse-stall, but didn't mean to remain that way.

'I'm considering!' he shouted back. Adding under his breath, 'You women-killing slime!'

Before he made his play he had to give her a little more time to reach the top. If he didn't made it to the horse, and didn't get up there to join her as a result, then at least she'd be out of sight, be in a position to run.

He wondered grimly how long she might last if that was the case. The men down there behind the sixguns were manhunters by trade. And there were four of them.

A freezing snowflake touched his cheekbone as he double-checked his Colts and took a last look at his plan. It was full of 'ifs'. If Hannah could reach the cliff top and wait for him; if he could make it down to his horse, circle round the cliff and pick her up without getting sieved; if . . . He shook his head. Don't Jonah yourself, dude. Time to move out.

He dropped belly-flat and began making his slow wriggling way along the trail ledge. Soon the old cabin lay well behind, creaking in the wind. He could still dimly make out tree and shrub shapes below, which meant they in turn would see him if he got careless. He hugged the stone passionately. No sounds from above now, thankfully no sound of a plummeting body.

Then: 'What are you playin' at, government man? You quittin' or are we coming up after you?'

Dimitri's voice was laced with impatience. Snatching a lightning peek over the edge, Duke tried to place the voice with the hope of loosing half a dozen bullets its way. But of the lumbering Southerner with the alien name there was no sign.

These bastards were good. Stood to reason. A man in Singleman's position could afford the best. He knew he believed the girl's story from beginning to end; it was too ugly to be anything but authentic. And it all tied in with the current political situation. With Singleman a hot candidate for the biggest job in the Territory, the big man simply couldn't risk the late Attorney North's daughter popping up with her story and her damning evidence to destroy not only his political ambitions but likely land him on Prison Island for ninety-nine years, or the gibbet.

Gun-running for the Cheyennes at a time when the Indian wars were setting the frontier aflame was about as heinous a crime any man could commit.

Duke meant to see Singleman pay in full for every single crime, including tonight. But it wasn't going to be handed to him on a platter. He must earn that right.

Sweating now despite the chill, he reached the point he'd earmarked as the most likely spot from which to make his descent. He glanced up. For some reason, and despite the onset of evening and the overlay of weather, he saw it was still not completely dark.

What to do? Risk climbing down some twenty feet to the cover? Or jump?

He shook his head. A man could break a leg taking the latter course. On the other hand, it would have to take ten, maybe as much as fifteen seconds to clamber down. More than enough time for him to get shot into doll-rags, if spotted.

From the crash of that first close shot, he'd known who it was out there, who it had to be. The name dropped by Silleck up at the Whiskey Shack had connected the entire bunch to the shootout in Prairie Valley, and from that moment on he'd known it could only be a matter of time before the game they were playing turned into a war.

The gang must already have been close on his hammer after he stopped by at Poor Town earlier. He'd made no attempt to conceal his tracks. No time. It figured they'd trailed him, closed in where their deadly marksmanship and Silleck's voice had confirmed his worst fears. Now the odds were stacked against him. But he had to believe he was better at this than they were, which maybe improved the odds more towards an even-money bet. Or was that just a case of an inveterate and optimistic gambler shaping the odds his way?

Whatever, he knew he'd still be one relieved field man to put this place which Hannah had called Cliff Gulch behind him with a full skin.

He stiffened sharply. Rustling movement drifting

in his direction from the brush below. Make-up-your-mind-time, field man.

Without hesitation he sprang erect and jumped.

A sixgun began churning from someplace off to his right as he plummeted down, but he didn't even hear a slug strike stone, much less come close.

He couldn't picture a Dimitri or a Silleck missing at that range, most likely the liquored-up *hombre* he'd punched in the teeth. Or so he figured as he hit ground, rolled three times then plunged headlong into the enveloping woods. That heller looked a loser, which a man couldn't rightly say about Dimitri or Silleck. He wondered who the other man was who'd arrived here with them, bringing the odds up to four-to-one against.

That thought was a spur and he tore between clutching trees at breakneck speed, head tucked low and Colt at the ready. Two shots whipped his way before he reached the horse, one whistling menacingly close. And now, as he fitted foot to stirrup and swung up, they were barking to one another through the darkness, like hunting dogs.

'He's cuttin' west towards that high yeller tree, Dimitri. Be ready to stop him busting back out the way he came in!'

'He's nearer the creek!' argued a big bass voice. 'Brodie, git across there and if you see anything, shoot it!'

No response from Brodie. Could be in too much of a funk for hooting and hollering. But all that signified right now was that he had his horse underneath him, and all three voices were away off to his right someplace, so he reckoned his odds had just firmed considerably.

He kicked hard once and went storming through the snowy woods, hoofs churning up great clumps of damp turf. Following the stream line for a short distance, he reached the sentinel shape of the lightning-struck white pine he'd pinpointed from the cliff. From this point there was a fold between the hills curving back eastward which would, he hoped, take him up to the cliff top, where he prayed he would find her waiting.

It did, and she was.

Just a handful of minutes later saw a hard-breathing Montana holster his gun and reach down to swing the remarkably composed girl up behind him. The split second she was astride he kicked again and, as though sensing the urgency and danger, the good horse rocketed away like a Derby winner, hoofs barely seeming to touch ground.

As they continued to roar through the forest at breakneck speed, ducking reaching branches and veering away from gopher holes and broken ground, often at the very last split second, Hannah North was plastered to his back, arms locked about his middle. Whenever he spoke her reply was calm, but through the clothing he could feel her heart going like a triphammer.

He had a hunch his own wasn't any slower. It was at times like this he truly believed that, despite the generous salaries they commanded, every Bureau field man was criminally underpaid.

He filled in the racing miles mapping out his plans

for when they reached town.

Cussing and tetchy, Ramont was weaving just a little as he locked up the main street office, then shook hands with the padlock to ensure it was secure. Not that he really gave a damn, or so he told himself as he paused to touch a vesta flame to the cigarette jutting from his teeth.

Just yesterday he'd considered Bella generous when she'd airily handed over the business to him leaving herself free to concentrate on staging her three or four big shows a week at the Palace, which were hauling in the paying customers by the score.

Tonight he wasn't so sure. For while the office kept him in constant contact with the the miners, and, as a consequence, he was getting a pretty good handle on what was happening up in the Dogwoods – which would lead to good money in time – even without Bella around to sweet-talk the boneheads and con them into signing up for far more than they could rightly afford, he could envision profits plummeting in next to no time.

'Bitch!' he muttered, and thrust his hands deep in the pockets of his navy-blue seaman's jacket and went looking for another drink.

He knew he wasn't cut out for business, even crooked business. He was a two-fisted fringe dweller whose only real specialties were dancing, brawling and winning women.

He'd been proud he'd won Bella – or thought he had. But the first time Duke the dude had given her the look he'd become yesterday's news. She'd kicked

him out of the Palace, placated him with the business
– goodbye, that's all, she wrote.

So naturally he drank. It helped calm him down. It
also seemed to help him keep patience with the
thickest, worst-smelling breed of humankind on this
planet, namely the miners he had to deal with.

He'd covered a half-block on the snow-slippery
walks before finding himself slowing, then stopping.
He stood with his head tilted to one side as he
massaged the inside of his wrists to sharpen his
senses. He wasn't a clever man but he was an intuitive
one. Instinct told him that there was something
different about the pulsebeat of Hellfire tonight,
something in the very air. He could feel it. It briefly
excited him, but then he just shrugged, shoved his
hands in his pockets and strolled on.

Whatever was tingling through the air of Wagon
Street tonight it likely wouldn't get to do anything for
him.

He stopped on a dime before the lamplit front
porch of the cramped little four-bed hospital and
doctor's surgery. Bella was just emerging, pretty as a
hand filled with aces, rugged up in a fur-collared
coat.

' 'Night, Klondyke!' he heard her call. 'See you
tomorrow!'

He stepped back into the shadows so as not to be
seen as she danced down the steps and hurried off.

'What a phony!' he muttered, spitting his half-
smoked cigarette into the gutter. There she was dancing attention on that hairy-assed miner Montana had
brought in from the hills with a shirtful of broken

ribs. Bella, the ministering angel! What a crock! She wouldn't visit the sick in a fit. Either she reckoned that smelly bum had the gold he was always spruiking about, or else she was cooking up some slippery scheme where she figured she could make use of him. Nobody could tell him anything about Bella Duvall.

Yet if he really hated her so much, why did it feel so bad to watch her disappearing in the crowd?

Might as well tie one on at the Palace, he decided. Maybe later he could go hiss her some when she appeared on stage with her all-girl revue of half-naked tarts. Bitch!

He'd never really expected to hold onto a woman like that for too long, he knew. It was losing her to Montana that really galled.

Ramont was flash but Montana was flasher. He was tough but that dude had walked all over him. Now he'd just crooked a finger and had Bella back in tow, pretending it was all a bit of mining-town fun, when Buck Ramont knew she was genuinely starry-eyed about that mucker.

A shambling drunk jostled him and Ramont seized him by the collar and punched the side of his head to send him spinning off the plankwalk, passers-by jumping clear.

'What are you lookin' at?' he snarled at them, feeling his power. He gestured. 'Step aside and let a man through. Why should I walk round the likes of you.'

Obediently the night-crawlers made an avenue and he was swaggering through it when he saw a familiar figure approaching the other way.

Had he been sharper he might have realized

131

immediately that the drifter Silleck looked anything but his regular cocky and self-satisfied self, and appeared to be riding a high-voltage mean streak as he propped to glare after a passer-by, then shoved another roughly out of his path as he came on with that catlike, graceful step.

'Howdy, pard.'

Ramont's greeting was amiable. He liked dangerous company and this man was that in spades. Despite Ramont's profile as Bella's ex, a damned fine dancer, good with his fists and a hit with a certain breed of percentage girl, his street rating was solid but not high. Silleck, by contrast, was the real McCoy, and looked it, every inch. Still very much a mystery figure about town, the man appeared to drift in and out at odd times, was sometimes to be seen in strange company; you might encounter him riding alone on an empty trail at three in the morning and never have a notion what he was about.

In short, exactly the kind that a go-getter like Ramont would like to pard up with to lend him cred. So he grinned, spread his hands and suggested they go take a shot, his treat, of course.

'Why don't you get out of my way before I sit you on your ass, tap-dancer?'

Ramont paled. Silleck was never exactly pally, but he'd never been hostile before.

He stepped aside hastily. 'Sorry, just thought that mebbe . . .' Ramont's voice faltered for Silleck looked not merely peeved, but downright lethal.

'Freakin' losers!' the hardcase hissed, was moving on when he suddenly paused, stared at Ramont over

his shoulder, came back. Ramont was in a panic.
Judas! All he'd done was suggest a drink!

'Ramont, ain't it?'

'Yeah. Buck. Look, man I didn't mean to get you
sore—'

'She dumped you and shacked with the dude.
Right?'

Ramont blinked. 'Er, Bella, you mean. Well, yeah,
I guess you could say that—'

'Where is she now? Come on, come on, I'm askin'
and you're answerin'. Where's your double-dealin'
slut right now, tap-dancer?'

'Why, matter of fact I just seen her on the street.'

'By herself?' He nodded and the man demanded:
'Where's Montana?'

'Heck, I dunno, man. Should I?'

Silleck appeared to be thinking hard, his eyes
never leaving his. Abruptly he reached out and
draped a lean arm around Ramont's shoulders, gave
a little squeeze.

'Look, er . . . Buck, I was just a tad tetchy there.
Got a lot on my mind. Truth of it is, I'm lookin' for
that fancy-fingered card-sharp tonight, need to find
him real bad. I checked out his hotel then looked
over the Palace, but nobody's seen a sign. For damn
good reasons, he's tryin' to dodge me. But I've got
even bigger reasons to want to find him. He's got a
dame with him and he ain't goin' to find it easy to
hide 'em both, so it could be he's gonna need help.
Why, he might even turn to that blonde you and him
trade hand to hand. Gettin' the way I'm thinkin',
amigo?'

133

Ramont wasn't nervous any longer. Suddenly this man was treating him like an equal, a pard even. What was even more encouraging was the realization that Silleck and Montana had had some sort of falling out, and this gave him a twinge of excitement. He doubted he could get on top of Montana, but if anyone could it was yellow-eyed Silleck.

'Tell me more . . .' he began, then broke off as someone halted at his side.

'Well, this is a pretty pair,' growled Sheriff Dunstan. 'A man does his level best to keep his town up to scratch, but all he sees are shady characters and guntippers and Lord knows what else—'

'How would you like to shift your raggedy ass before I put a bullet through it, lawdog?'

Ramont backed up a pace, shocked by Silleck's recklessness. Dunstan was shocked also, and for a moment it appeared that Hellfire's tough peace officer would react. Dunstan wanted to stand tough, knew he should. What stopped him was the expression on Silleck's face. The man's eyes blazed fire and his mouth was hooked down at one side, lending him a slightly crazy look. He also had one hand resting on gunbutt, and both Ramont and Dunstan sensed that he just might be ready to use it.

It was at that exact moment that the lawman knew he'd outlasted his time. He'd sensed his authority dwindling in recent days. Now this man standing before him with the snow drifting down behind him was telling him in a way far clearer than words that it was gone.

Head down, the lawman turned and walked on,

leaving Ramont sleeving his brow.

'Whew! You sure got a way of gettin' your point across, Silleck.'

'You want to help a man out or don't you, Ramont?' Silleck was all business again.

'Why, er . . . well, hell, I guess I do.' Ramont studied the other a moment, then grinned. 'Hell no, I know I do. If that double-dealin' jade wants to play hard card, two can play it. Tell me what I can do to help you find that motherless dude, pal.'

Which was howcome Buck Ramont, sober now even though he'd rather be drunk, found himself some thirty minutes later creeping up the back stairs at the Silver Palace, on his way along the landing until reaching the single back window of Bella Duvall's suite, where he halted nervously and found himself reaching up with a hand that trembled for the broken shutter clasp he knew to be there.

CHAPTER 9

COLT HEAT

Bella hummed softly to herself as she walked along the carpeted hallway and inserted the silver key into the doorlock of her suite of rooms.

Palace employees of years standing resented her being given the best rooms in the place after barely a week on the payroll. But she had Chett Wilson wrapped round her little finger from the outset, far less by the magic of her charms than the dollars-and-cents reality that she'd almost doubled his custom and earnings with her spectacular shows downstairs.

With the kind of confidence only a woman like Bella possessed, she knew she would have won the suite, the salary and the attention with or without the shows – which were beginning bore her anyway.

Bella bored easily, even felt half-way bored tonight after returning from the hospital. She was a woman who thrived on the new, the unexpected, the romantic and the challenging. Upon her arrival in town she'd set up the claims office and taken over the entertainment at the Palace inside twenty-four hours. Since then she'd reunited with the only man she'd ever loved and shown another admirer the door, which reminded her that she hadn't sighted Duke all day. As she stepped into the apartment and stopped on a dime.

Confronting her were two people who'd just completed a ten-mile hike through the snow. They were wet and bedraggled yet still made an impressive spectacle, the male half of which couldn't have been a more welcome sight.

'Duke? What in the name . . . ?'

'No time, honey,' he said soberly, coming to give her a squeeze. He indicated his companion. 'Bella, Hannah North, Hannah, meet—'

'The girl you've been searching for?' Bella cried. She extended her hand and Hannah took it. 'Your fingers are like ice, Hannah. Duke, what have you been doing to this poor girl?'

She was light-hearted, but not for long. By the time Montana quit the suite just a short time later, a very sober Bella had learned all about Hannah North, her father, the killings, her flight and the two years incognito in Hellfire. What she understood most clearly was the current situation which had seen Montana forced to seek her assistance in concealing the girl from a pack of killers while he sought help.

Generous by nature, Bella accepted the request without a moment's hesitation, even was excited by it all, as Montana had suspected she would be. He also knew he was leaving Hannah in the safest of hands as he danced downstairs and took the back way out to go looking for his superior.

He found Polk in the brightly lit dining-room of his hotel. He was seated alone working his way through the grilled salmon and parsley sauce. English tweeds and impeccable manners caused him to stand out even in this fairly stylish crowd.

Montana had managed to clean himself up some on his way from the saloon, but was still a long way short of his regular impeccable self, with torn shirt, sodden boots and his hair plastered to his head. But the self-assurance bordering on arrogance was still evident as he strode directly across the room, turning every head before banging his knuckles down on an astonished Polk's table.

'Come on, we've got to talk,' he stated.

'My dear fellow, as you can see I'm in the middle of—'

'I've found her!' Montana hissed, leaning close. 'I've got her stashed but there's a bunch of gunpackers on our hammer. C'mon, we'll go see the sheriff, muster some men and . . .' He broke off. Polk had resumed eating. 'What the hell . . . ? Didn't you hear what I said?'

'Assuredly.' Polk chewed. 'Mmm, good salmon.' He swallowed. 'But as usual, you've acted totally outside guidelines without approval or proper planning, Montana. You were supposed first to locate our party, then report back to me and wait for me to receive word from the Bureau as to the best method of extricating her without attracting attention or publicity, certainly without violence. I'm afraid this is a problem of your own making, and you will simply have to cope with it as best you can until I can contact the Bureau and receive further instruction.'

Montana's face was a study. It would have been laughable were it not so hair-raisingly real. The world of investigation, as seen through this man's blink-ered vision, was orderly, sensible and disciplined and operated strictly by the manual. Whereas in reality it could often be chaotic, totally unpredictable and murderously dangerous. Like tonight.

'Look, you pompous son of a bitch,' he hissed. 'You get up out of that fat chair and—'

'You're becoming offensive and tedious, Montana,' Polk snapped, waving his hand. 'You're Dismissed.'

Montana turned away. He continued to turn until he faced the table again. He seized hold of it with both hands then upturned it to take Polk, the salmon, the sauce, the freshly opened bottle of red wine and clattering shower of glassware and cutlery to the floor with him.

'There goes the job,' he muttered, leaving the room at the trot. But that was the least of his concerns. He'd not sighted the gunmen out on the trail but knew they would figure he'd return to town; it was the only place he could come. They'd have to be out searching for him right now. And her. He didn't know how much time he might have left.

Whatever he had, it was several minutes less by the time he'd detoured to the law office. He left alone moments later. The sheriff was absent, had gone home ill according to the deputy. Naturally the deputy couldn't leave the office unmanned. Hellfire? A better name would be Yellowville.

His mind raced as he headed back for the Silver Palace. He'd planned to have Polk and the sheriff muster a citizens' posse, firstly to ensure Hannah's safety, and secondly to deal with the gang. Instead he was on his own, and was conjuring up and discarding one possible hideaway after another, as he cut along St Leque and took the main street for the saloon.

The two-story Palace building loomed before him against the shifting skies.

'Maybe the diggings?' he was thinking as he cut around in back for the rear stairs, but realized he was grabbing at straws. He'd have to come up with something more practical than that.

He jolted to a halt in the half-darkness, his breath cutting short.

A shadowy figure was swiftly climbing the stairs, a beam of window-light catching fire along the barrel of the gun in his fist. It was the man he'd slugged up at the Whiskey Shack, Brodie.

Cutting his gaze higher, he glimpsed a second man on the balcony, head and shoulders silhouetted against the square of light that was one of Bella's windows.

That silhouette was large and menacing, even at distance. Dimitri.

'Light someplace, I said!'

August's tone was soft but carried weight. Bella shrugged and seated herself on the arm of the ottoman where Hannah was seated, toying nervously with the tassels on a cushion.

The suite directly above the casino comprised

140

three rooms and a large clothes'-closet around half room size, with a window overlooking the rear yard. The living-room was spacious and needed to be so on a night like this with six adults occupying it. The bedroom opened onto the living-room. There was nobody in there and August had the key to it in his pocket. He didn't want anyone disappearing on him here. The third room was a utility room-cum-eatery-cum-sewing-room where Bella stitched up some of her special costumes. It was hung with glitzy outfits which Dimitri was studying gloomily as he munched his way through a chicken-and-mustard on rye, heavy jaws working hard, a hogleg sixshooter thrusting up from the waistband of his britches.

Low man in the pecking-order, Brodie was the only one of the gang out of August's sight, having been relegated to keeping watch on the out-back from the wardrobe room window.

The window had proved the suite's Achilles heel for Bella and her charge.

Having shared the quarters with Bella before receiving his marching orders, Ramont had known about the broken latch. He'd run out of bravado immediately after checking it out to ensure it had not been repaired, but by then he had done what was required of him.

The two women had been seated at the mahogany table in the front room when Silleck appeared soundlessly in the utility room doorway with a Colt .45 in his fist, smirking like the cat that ate the cream and panting a little from the swift ascent of the outside stairs and the climb through the window.

Now the killer paced cat-footed in and out and up and down, while August, seated at the table with a Peacemaker on a linen napkin before him, studied the women and did his thinking out loud.

'He should have got back by now. Where'd you say he was going when he left here, sister?'

'I didn't say.'

Bella was the coolest of the entire six. This fact would not have surprised Montana, had he been present, but it impressed the gang boss, to his annoyance.

'So, as I get it, you were with Montana way back when. He dumped you, you met up on the last stage when you were with the tap-dancer, you all checked in here, then you kicked your tap-dancer out and took up with the dude again? Pretty free and easy, aren't you, sister?'

'He's not coming back here,' Bella said coolly, getting up to move around again despite Silleck's warning look. 'I know that much.'

'Sure you do,' Silleck said with heavy irony. 'The dude spends weeks huntin' for this dame, kills a couple of guys doin' it, finds her and damn near gets both of them killed gettin' her back here to town – then just walks out and doesn't bother comin' back. I'll swallow that, even if nobody else would. The hell I would!'

He stopped by the table and dropped his sarcastic manner. 'We can't freakin' stay here, Kurt. The son of a bitch could be out there rustlin' up half the town—'

'He doesn't even know we're here, damnit!'

August snapped.

'He ain't stupid. He'd figure we'd come back here. I say, let's finish the skirt right now and get the hell out of here.'

'What about the papers?' August replied. 'Those documents they never found when her old man got croaked. Remember? The big man said when we found her we had to make her cough up the documents just in case she'd been smart enough to make sure they came to light even if we killed her. Don't you remember anything?'

The Bowie knife leapt into Silleck's lean hand as though conjured there. Two steps took him to the ottoman. Hannah's eyes were like saucers as the blade tip touched her neck, drawing blood. The killer glared back over his shoulder at August, who'd risen.

'She's either gonna tell us about the papers or I'm gonna slit her dumb throat right here and now. I'm not lookin' to set here like some dumbass waitin' for half the town to come through that door. So, all right, you bitch do what—'

He broke off at a strange sound from the next room. All turned to see Brodie coming in from the darkened wardrobe closet, walking rigidly, eyes like saucers.

Dimitri dropped his food, cursed, stared at his henchman.

'What's wrong with you, dummy . . . ?'

There was the sound of a heavy blow. Brodie's eyes rolled in their sockets as he pitched forward, stiff as a board, to smash face downwards into the floor, revealing the grim-faced man with twin Colt .45s in his hands standing behind him.

'Duke!'

Montana's guns exploded with an ear-shattering roar that engulfed Bella's cry. Dimitri took the double charge squarely in the chest, food erupting from his mouth upon a geyser of dark blood. His big body slammed sideways into the table and broke it in half with a sound like another gunshot as he fell to the floor.

Montana dropped on one knee and pivoted, looking for Silleck before realizing the killer had dived in back of the ottoman. From the corner of his eye, he caught August snatching up the Peacemaker, lips pulled back from big teeth in a feral snarl, sweeping the barrel around.

Duke shot the ringleader through the right eye and killed him where he sat. While the body was still twitching from the bullet in the brain, Duke started coming up, ready to hurl himself past Bella to reach the ottoman, then realized it was too late.

Hannah was now standing. But it wasn't voluntary. Silleck stood behind her with his sixgun protruding from under her left breast, the tip of a big skinning-knife against her throat again.

'Drop 'em, dude!' the killer hissed. He pressed the knife and a trickle of blood showed. 'Now!'

The twin Colts hit the floor as Montana slowly straightened. 'Leave her be and I'll see you get out of here alive. You've got my word.'

'Lyin' bastard!'

Silleck switched focus to Bella, who still looked

totally calm, standing there with her pocketbook in her hands now as though ready to step out and go shopping.

'You. Get to the door, bitch. Fast. And you're comin' with us, dude. Treble insurance.' He jerked the gun at Bella. 'Move!'

Bella did as ordered. Hannah didn't cry out, didn't make a sound. Her body was slack and her eyes were pools of terror slanting up at the edges. She wasn't breathing.

Calmly, Bella reached the door and worked the lock to open it. Mounting sounds of alarm could be heard from the corridor. She took one step back and caught Montana's eye. She nodded.

Duke was slow to catch on. Silleck was now backing for the door, eyes flicking from one to the other. He was starting to grin like a dog wolf.

'Come on, dude, you keep by me close. We're all goin' out together like one happy family, and you're gonna tell all those rubes just to stand back quiet and calm and mind their own damn business on account you know there ain't no way I can't take you both down if they do anythin' else. Move!'

Montana glanced back to Bella, who rested a hand on her pocketbook. Now the nickel dropped. She wanted to get at that pistol, wanted him to distract Silleck.

He immediately lunged at the outlaw, snarling and cursing. Surprised momentarily, the desperado recovered fast. Now the gun was in Montana's face. He saw the finger whitening on the trigger. But he went on raging and waving his arms. Bella's hand vanished inside the pocketbook. Silleck didn't turn. The hammer of his gun was beginning to lift. An eternal second. Sweat erupted on Montana's brow. Then a stab of boreflame erupted through the black leather and Silleck and the girl were punched forward by the impact of hot lead smashing into living flesh and bone. Lightning-fast, Montana shot out an arm to prevent the girl from falling, thereby making room for the dead killer to hit the floor face down, a fist-sized hole in the back of his skull.

Pandemonium erupted in the corridor. People began pouring through the door into a room wreathed in gunsmoke. But Bella and the Duke only had eyes for each other.

CHAPTER 10

THE MIDNIGHT SPECIAL

She kissed him full on the lips and Montana felt that old familiar feeling. Then he remembered who it was he was kissing and told the old feeling to get lost.

'I'll be beholden to you for as long as I live, Duke,' she promised, all dimples and sparkling eyes as she stood in the train doorway. 'Who knows, I might even name my first son after you.'

'Take care, Hannah North,' he smiled, and stepped back as the engineer blew his whistle to set the Westbound rolling.

What a girl, he mused, strolling through the depot gate. She'd seen her father murdered and endured years in exile from friends and family in fear of her life as a result. Yet she'd never given up on her vow to bring to justice the man responsible, and had stayed on here in Hellfire long enough to see that happen.

The headline of the newspaper tucked under his

147

arm as he headed for the hotel, screamed:

SINGLEMAN TO FACE GRAND JURY

The sometimes slow hand of the law had moved with surprising speed once the county attorney received the metal case containing every shred of damning documented evidence Hannah's late father had amassed against Singleman, surely one of the most corrupt power-brokers the Territory had ever produced.

Even punctilious Polk had pronounced the evidence 'incontrovertible'. He now predicted this testimony would be supported by Hannah North's eyewitness account of her father's murder by men under Singleman's direct command, could well see the would-be territorial governor receive – instead of the endorsement of the Territory at the polls – life or the rope.

Made a man feel proud to have played a part in his downfall. But as usual at times like this, mostly what field man Montana experienced was a sharp sense of anticlimax, that sudden and painful withdrawal from the two things he craved the most. Excitement and money. Well, three if he counted Bella. And who but an idiot wouldn't count a somebody like her.

He found Polk waiting in the dining-room, seated at the very same table Montana had buried him under in an earlier, more turbulent moment.

The Bureau's personnel chief was all smiles, and that should have been a warning.

Polk promptly produced a glowing letter of

commendation for Investigator Montana signed personally by Chief Cullenmore. He assured his field man that, despite their differences, he'd enjoyed working with him and insisted on adding his own compliments concerning the way he'd stuck to his guns and seen the North case through despite setbacks, criticism and, in its closing stages, truly desperate danger.

'Um,' was Duke's response. He wasn't working at the moment but his work-honed instincts were still on duty, and were beginning to click in. They warned him the change in the Englishman was too dramatic to ring true.

Nonetheless, Polk maintained his smooth and cheerful manner right up to the moment Duke rose to leave for an appointment at the blackjack layout at the Silver Palace. Why, he even extended a big bony hand and shook his vigorously.

'I'm proud, Investigator Montana. Real proud. Oh, and by the way, you're on stand-down.' A huge, toothy smile as phony as a three-dollar bill. 'Indefinite stand-down.'

The bastard!

The bar clock had just struck ten but already the casino was half-empty. Hellfire had been force-fed more excitement than it could comfortably handle and now seemed to be succumbing belatedly to a kind of communal indigestion of exhaustion. By the weekend things should be looking up, but nothing much was likely to revive this misting October's night.

So thought almost everybody in the Palace with the exception of the noisy old miner from the Dogwood Hills doing his best to liven up both the lonelies at the bar, and the stylish couple gloomily sipping rum punches well back from the pinecone fire.

'To good times and better understandings,' Duke Montana toasted.

'Well, good times anyway.'

'Come, Bell, ease up. Just look at us. Chipper and chirpy, with money in our pockets and nothing but stardust on the horizon. Why so serious?'

'You never cease to amaze me, Montana . . .'

She looked a million dollars in a low-cut creation from Madame Zelda's, her hair piled high and precious stones glittering at wrist and throat. Yet her mood was strange, and for that matter, so was his.

There were increasing pauses, long silences, the occasional sigh. The dramas were over and the dust was settling. They'd been through hell and high water together, had bonded like a professional team, as indeed had been the case in Sun River. Now . . . peace and quiet.

But things should be livening up shortly. Bella was bored with Hellfire and had signed up for several weeks on stage in Tombstone, Arizona. She'd invited him to accompany her and he'd agreed. He had nothing to do until that evil-minded Polk relented and put him back on Operational.

He was showing signs of boredom also.

Another silence. Bella cleared her throat.

'Oh, congratulations on your award. I'm sure I

150

didn't congratulate you before, did I? You really are in a class of your own in your line of work, whatever that may be, Duke.'

'Obliged, Bell,' he said, taking out his special deck. He cocked an eyebrow. 'But it should have gone to you, by rights.' He winked. 'What are you doing the rest of the night?'

She smiled, soft dimples creasing the corners of her mouth, causing his pulse to kick, as only she could. Some things never changed.

'I'm not at all sure that's a genuine proposition, Montana. Maybe the past is overtaking us tonight.'

He frowned. She thought he was in an odd mood; he felt she was. He knew he was restless, damned restless. But he wasn't the only one. Unless there were fireworks and something new to excite her, Belle seemed to lose her edge as well. They were alike in so many ways. Maybe too alike.

He dismissed that thought and was manipulating the pack again when an all-too familiar voice intruded on yet another silence between them.

'Well, goddamn, just look at them, will you? Playin' cards and makin' moon eyes when they could be roarin' on their way to a fortune before daybreak. Fair breaks a man's heart, so it does. It's a crime.'

'Klondyke,' Bella sighed, as Montana groaned. 'We're both glad you're up and about and raring to go, honest. But tone down, will you. We're discussing the future here.'

'Now that's a coincidence!' the prospector said as he crossed from the bar. Then he dropped into a chair at their table and his voice dropped to a conspiratorial whisper. 'Couldn't you see I've been workin' my way round to gettin' to you folks ever since you came in.'

He held a finger to his lips as both made to speak at once, a wild-eyed leprechaun with breath to cripple a kitten.

'Act natural,' he commanded. 'I swear some of these parasites and predators can smell gold on a man's skin. And gold is what we're talkin' about this fine night, now ain't that right?'

Wrong.

And yet both knew they welcomed the interruption. Any interruption would be welcome for Bella and the Duke at that moment of 'peace and tranquility', which was beginning to get on their nerves. They were excitement addicts, and there seemed to be some aura of excitment about this crazy old Cousin Jack tonight.

He sat beaming at them both a moment. He regarded them as his only true friends now. Duke had saved his life and Bella had taken it on herself to pamper him through his recovery. They liked him despite his eccentricities, his endless failures to strike it rich.

'Look, Klon,' Montana began, but the man seized his wrist in a grip like iron.

'No, let me talk. I'm bustin'.' A tear glinted in his eye. 'That day on the OK, boy. When the bandits set upon me and busted my ribs and ripped up my clothin' lookin' for the gold they claimed I'd found. Do you know where it was?'

'There wasn't any gold, you old pan-washer!'

'No? Well, what's this then?'

Klondyke was seated with his back to the room. He now hunched over and plunged a hand into an inside pocket of his outsized weather jacket and hauled forth two solid gold nuggets the size of crab-apples.

Suddenly two sometime lovers weren't thinking about love and boredom anymore. They might not know a lot about mining, but both loved gold and could recognize the real thing on sight.

It was Duke who spoke first.

'This some kind of scam?'

'He doesn't scam,' Bella said soberly. 'What's this all about, Klon?'

The prospector looked crafty.

'Ah hah! Not so keen to see old Klondyke off now, are y—'

'Either start talking or vanish!' Montana snapped.

'Fine, I'll talk.'

It was a familiar tale. Lone miner prospects for years in the wilds someplace where he 'knows' he will strike it rich. He is laughed to scorn. He's secretive, suspicious and doesn't trust a living soul. Endless labor, privation and heartbreak as he grows old – then a chance swipe with a pickaxe reveals it. The vein. It's the real thing. He's rich. But the location is remote and difficult, extraction will require long and hard labor, he's surrounded by bandits and untold danger – at least in his own mind, and what he really needs is the help of people he can trust.

And he can't think of more than just two friends he's made in all his fifty-four years of hard-scrabbling, untrusting, busted-luck life.

This was the real thing. They could see this by his samples, the glowing assays he produced. It was waiting for them – for Klondyke and his two great friends. Maybe Bella could cook and mind camp while he and Duke got the whole thing set up. And when they'd cleaned up the vein – in just a few months – all three could retire to the Capital or Kansas City and spend, spend, spend until they died – the seam was that rich.

So, what did they say now?

Montana was suspicious. Not about the gold, for it was as pure as any he'd ever seen. But every scam started with gold. Were they being scammed?

'That day on the trail,' he said. 'Those bandits damn near stripped you naked and tore your pack apart. Where was the gold?'

Klondyke's leprechaun face split into a smile.

'Hammered flat and laid in the soles of my old workin' boots. Smart, huh?' His grin vanished. 'Trust me now, sonny?'

'We trust you, Klon,' said Bella, studying Montana. 'But I don't think we're really interested, are we, Duke?'

'Guess not.'

Had it taken him a second longer than it should have to answer? Was he having difficulty taking his eyes off the nuggets? Was he thinking too sharply about wandering around Tombstone with the Earps with empty pockets while Bella brought in the money?

Just what was he thinking?

Turned out neither was interested. The miner had half-expected Bella to turn him down, but was genuinely surprised when Montana also sat there shaking his head. He'd studied his Good Samaritan at close hand, had a powerful hunch that Duke was the kind who'd happily live on muddy water and sleep in a hollow log if it led to his climbing aboard the gold-train for life.

Seemed he was wrong.

'Sorry to disappoint you, old-timer. But who wants to winter in the high country with blizzards screeching and screaming down out of Canada all winter long anyway?'

It was a case of thanks, but no thanks. They were unanimous – or were they? When gold entered the equation with people who yearned for wealth as they did, it could prove difficult to be certain of anything.

Klondyke was crestfallen.

'OK, OK,' he sighed. 'You can keep them things as mementoes. I'll have bigger and better than them runnin' out my ears in a couple of weeks.' He rose to leave. 'But just in case you change your minds, I'm leavin' on the Midnight Special for the hills tonight, and the offer's still open 'til then . . .'

Walking Belle to her room upstairs a short time later, Duke Montana was deeply confused. He'd never felt closer to this woman. He'd had every intention of spending the night with her, but knew now he just couldn't do it. He was in a turmoil, excited and guilty all at once – but mostly excited.

He told her he needed a few more Godfathers to unwind. That he might then wander over to the

155

Territory and compose that letter to Cully, demanding reinstatement, maybe do some packing. Said he couldn't wait until they were on their way south together. Honest.

He was astonished when she seemed almost relieved.

'I understand, Duke. Kiss me goodnight.'

She stood framed in the doorway, the face and figure that drove men wild from the Mississippi to San Fran. Duke's expression was blank, but inside he was a volcano. He wanted her desperately in that moment, wanted her to want him, could feel the attraction between them stronger than it had ever been. Yet he still knew he wouldn't stay.

Couldn't.

'See you in the morning, honey.' His voice sounded hoarse.

'Love you.'

'You too.'

Again she seemed totally unconcerned as she smiled and shut the door in his face. Strange.

The latch clicked. Thank God. Another second and he might have started knocking.

He made it to the Territory in record time by horse-drawn cab. Had to. Time was running short. As he paused with his familiar carpetbag to check himself out in the full-length mirror – thinking that he looked sharp and stylish with maybe just a hint of something loco about his eyes, the sound of a distant train whistle touched him like a cattle prod.

The fifty-ton Titan loco and four-car train had already rolled in by the time he reached the depot.

Passengers were climbing on and off, mostly off. Only masochists with a really urgent desire to spend two hours clanking and snorting up the gradient to wind-driven Dogwood were left on board by the time he'd got his ticket and jumped aboard.

'Leavin' us already, Mr Montana?' the porter asked 'Too bad you can't stay a little longer, considerin' all what you done for us . . .'

Duke didn't even hear. Standing on the top steps, staring back at the lights of the town, he was saying goodbye to her and asking her to understand. Then, squaring his shoulders, adjusting the angle of his snappy hat and feeling the excitement pulsing through his bootsoles, he strode into the car.

A dozen-odd passengers occupied the thirty places available either side of the main car. At the far end of the brightly lit car was a padded cross-bench where people could sit with their backs to the loco, facing the car.

Seated in the center of this bench were two people staring straight at him as he came striding confidently through.

One was Klondyke.

The other was Bella.

'B'Gawd!' the prospector shouted, jumping to his feet. 'He's made it too, Miss Bella. Welcome aboard, boy. Changed your mind at the last minute? Prayed you would, son, just prayed you would.'

He could have been speaking Sanskrit for all he heard. Duke's stare was locked with hers as he came slowly forward. Those green eyes had never looked more like tempered steel. Worse, her pocket book lay on her lap, and her gloved hand was sliding into it.

'Why, Bell . . .' What could a man say?

'You bastard!'

She had no difficulty finding the right words. Suddenly every passenger was sitting up straight and paying attention, aware that something exciting was taking place, craning their necks to look from one figure to the other, nobody yet realizing the significance of that pocketbook, or the man's frozen smile.

'Bella, this isn't the way it looks—'

'I knew you were lying,' she accused. 'Even so, I prayed you wouldn't show up here. But I just had to come to make sure, something made me. And here you are. Couldn't help yourself, could you, you swine.'

'But, Bell honey, you're here too. And you said you weren't interested . . .'

She made some fierce retort that Duke didn't catch. He was distracted by Klondyke who had caught his attention and was furtively pointing downwards with a wicked glitter in his eyes.

Duke looked. He saw something blue protruding from beneath the seat. It looked familiar. Bella moved quickly to try and conceal it. But Montana wouldn't be denied, as suspicion hit. He thrust her aside, bent, grabbed a handle and came up with the blue leather valise she'd had with her the day he boarded the stage.

It weighed a ton. Packed to capacity if he was any judge.

And suddenly it was silent, the shrill sound of the conductor's whistle seeming faint and distant.

He stared at her accusingly. In turn she looked defensive, defiant, uncertain, eventually lifted a gloved hand to suppress a smile.

'You . . .' He was about to call her something, but remembered he was a gentleman. Above her glove, brilliant green eyes sparkled with excitement and mischief, but not a hint of repentance. He swallowed and started again, 'You were going without me . . .'

'So? You were going without me!'

'Who cares who was doin' what?' boomed Klondyke, jumping to his feet and flinging an arm around them both as the train jerked and began to move. 'What matters is we're all happy, we're together – and it's up there on the mountain just waitin' for us.'

The train gathered speed. Already too late to jump off. But did anyone want to? Montana was damned sure he didn't. And looking at her and realizing she was every bit as unpredictable, tricky and yes, maybe selfish as he was, felt a thrill of understanding course right through him.

They were crazy about one another but needed more than that to survive, he realized. Five or six days of harmony and boredom had proved that. They needed to be unsure, on the edge, and maybe even in constant danger – as they most likely would be working the claim – if it was to stay fresh for them. Suddenly it was all so clear.

Someone began to clap as they sat down side by side. Montana shoved the blue bag beneath the seat alongside his own. Klondyke beamed like a patriarch surrounded by his family.

159

He leaned back against the cushions and drew something from an inside pocket.

'Two hours to the Dogwoods . . . lots of time to kill.'

She slipped her arm through his. She smelt of roses.

'Pick a card,' he murmured, smiling at long last. 'Any card.'

She picked. It was the two of hearts.